"Are you telling me you're unhappy? That you want a change?"

"Maybe." Claire stepped away, where he wouldn't confuse her. "I guess I want to change the partnership a little."

She turned around and looked into Ben's warm, dark eyes. If she weren't careful, this argument would end with him promising plenty, changing nothing and romancing her into complacency.

"But I look at you and still see the sweet thing I married. And I promised to honor you, protect you and cherish you."

That sounded like a caveman talking.

"But you didn't promise to treat me like a child! Your sweet young thing is all grown up. And she's got a lot more sense than you give her credit for!"

Books by Lynn Bulock

Love Inspired

Gifts of Grace #80
Looking for Miracles #97
Walls of Jericho #125

LYNN BULOCK

lives in Thousand Oaks, California, with her husband and two sons, a dog and a cat. She has been telling stories since she could talk and writing them down since fourth grade. She is the author of nine contemporary romance novels.

Walls of Jericho
Lynn Bulock

Love Inspired

Published by Steeple Hill Books™

STEEPLE HILL BOOKS

Steeple
Hill™

ISBN 0-373-87132-5

WALLS OF JERICHO

Copyright © 2001 by Lynn M. Bulock

Visit us at www.steeplehill.com

Printed in U.S.A.

And we know that in all things God works for the good of those who love Him who have been called according to His purpose.

—Romans 8:28

To Joe, always

And
To my parents, Walter and Betty Hosea,
a truly matched pair

Chapter One

It was going to be a lovely wedding. Claire Jericho was sure of it. Now, if she could just marshal the troops to get there in time she could *enjoy* her father's lovely wedding.

Was she the only one in the whole extended family who could get ready on time? She paced the living room, hearing the click of her heels on the hardwood floor. She could hear the boys thumping around upstairs. Her two had the vague excuse of adding their cousin to the normal chaos of getting ready. But Ben had no excuse at all, and Laurel had their father's whole apartment to herself to get ready in. Where was she?

Running late or trying to replace panty hose at the last moment, Claire told herself. Old habits died hard. She could still remember the bathroom mirror wars when all three girls were at home, in this same house. Laurel was always the last one ready, no matter how much time they gave her.

Carrie, of course, was first. But then she had to be talked into wearing something better than jeans, a ball cap and T-shirt, which made the whole process last twice as long. And while her parents squabbled with Carrie, or tried to hurry Laurel along, Claire quietly got ready for whatever event they were going to.

Most of the time, it was church at Friedens Community Chapel—where they were all heading today if the rest of them ever got ready. She picked a tiny piece of lint off the skirt of her pink dress, and sighed. "Come on. We don't have all day."

As if Laurel had actually heard Claire for a change, she came through the front door. "Sorry it took this long. I put a run through the first pair of panty hose with my fingernail." She waggled her bright fuchsia nails. "Not used to these most of the time. They are elegant, though, aren't they?"

"Definitely." And probably cost more than Claire's weekly grocery bill. California was far different from Friedens, for sure. Laurel looked elegant from head to toe, with her brown hair in a perfect chignon, slim suit the same shade as her nails, and gorgeous pumps in a shade Claire couldn't even describe.

Her sister saw her looking at the shoes. "Yeah, I know, they're a bit much. But everybody says gray is going to be the new neutral for a couple seasons. I saw them at the mall and bought them before I thought about them. Would you believe that I actually had them halfway home, ready to show them to Sam, before I remembered—" Laurel's voice trailed off and her eyes filled with tears.

"Okay, now don't smear the makeup," Claire said, grabbing a tissue out of the side pocket of her dress. That was one of the reasons she'd worn this pale pink one. It had pockets, and she knew she'd need them to fill with tissues. But she hadn't thought she'd need them until church. "We said we'd get through this without thinking about Mom or Sam or any of those things."

Laurel's lip trembled. "I know. And I really meant it." She ran the backs of both hands up her cheeks. "There. I'm done. Now let's see where those guys are."

"I think they're about to find us." Claire could hear somebody marching down the stairs. It was a lighter step than usual, but all four males upstairs had traded their usual athletic shoes for something dressier today. The sounds rounded the bend to the landing, and shiny black loafers with pinstriped pant legs came into view. That had to be Ben.

Claire's heart still lifted at the sight of her husband. He looked so fine dressed up. He looked pretty good in the khakis and shirt he wore to work most days, but this was even better.

"It's about time," she told him. "You're supposed to set an example for the rest of that bunch. I thought I was going to have to come drag all of you down."

His grin was brighter than the sunshine streaming in the windows. And when he smiled like that, the same dimple appeared in his left cheek that she could trace now in Trent and Kyle.

"What if I don't want to set a good example?" Ben got to the bottom of the staircase and put his arms around her waist. "What if I want to kiss you, instead? You look wonderful. How much of my money did you spend on that new dress?"

"None, silly. Because it isn't new."

He held her at arm's length. "I'd remember that one from before, wouldn't I?" His slightly wolfish grin suggested that the dress was as flattering as she'd hoped.

"Honest, it's not new. I've, uh, enhanced it a little," Claire said.

"New jewelry? Different belt?" He was still holding her around the waist, and it made Claire want to squirm slightly, combined with the way he was still admiring her.

"Try about ten pounds less inside the dress," Laurel piped up from across the room. "Or does it take another woman to recognize that?"

Ben shrugged. "Whatever. It looks great, Claire. Want me to holler at the guys to get them down here?"

"Only if I get to cover my ears first," Laurel told him. "I remember your hollering, Ben Jericho. And it could shatter glass."

Claire braced herself for the ruckus she knew would erupt when Ben called the troops. At least this way they'd get to church on time.

Thirty minutes later everybody had made it the half block to church. With a minimum of fuss, they were all seated in the front pew, on the groom's side. As the organ music played and the minister spoke, Claire sat and helped her sister work through a whole purse-size package of tissues. "This is silly," she whispered as they stood for prayers. "I couldn't be happier."

It was a gorgeous June day. Sun streamed in the stained glass windows like a blessing, and the church was filled. Everything was going just right. But she was still crying. At least she wasn't alone. She could hear sniffling down the aisles behind her. Weddings just seemed to naturally do that to people. Women, at least.

"Me, too. We just show it oddly, I guess," Laurel said wryly. "The wonders of waterproof mascara." She fished another tissue out of the package and dabbed at her eyes. "Daddy looks so happy."

"He really does. I didn't think this would ever happen." Claire watched her father, beaming as he faced Gloria at the altar. It was amazing to Claire that after nearly a decade of being on his own, Hank had found someone to share his life with again.

He'd grieved long and hard after her mom had died from cancer. Who could have imagined that at sixty-one he'd be a bridegroom again? But it felt so right. Gloria was such a sweetheart. And she was so thrilled to have "lots of girls," as she put it. Claire could understand that. It was nice having another female around the house this weekend, even if it was her big sister, and only for a few days.

The couple looked more than happy. Hank still cut a dashing figure in a tuxedo. But then, he even looked good in his usual sheriff's uniform. And Claire had never seen Gloria look anything less than perfect, even when she was tending to her grandchildren. The pearl-gray suit she wore now fit her to perfection, and her wrist corsage of roses and baby orchids was luscious.

There was a shifting down the row, and Claire started to turn her head to see what her awful boys were getting up to. Laurel put a hand on top of hers. "Don't look. You really don't want to. I know that between yours and mine, they're doing something horrid. Just nudge Ben and have him take care of it."

That brought a smile to Claire's face. Ben handle the disturbance? Her husband was the biggest boy of all. He was probably in on whatever those hooligans down the row were doing. As was their Aunt Carrie, most likely. Her baby sister was never much for either romance or decorum. Even a wedding was not likely to change that. At least they'd talked her into wearing a dress. That sight itself might have set the boys off. They'd probably had no idea Carrie had legs.

Still, it wouldn't hurt to give Laurel's suggestion a try. "Ben?" she called softly. "Sit on whatever those guys are doing, okay?" She reached out to squeeze his arm and get his attention, in case her words hadn't. Good old solid Ben—her rock since she was no older than her fourteen-year-old nephew Jeremy.

"Right," Ben whispered back, leaning over her. His lips brushed her ear, making Claire shiver a little. His touch still did that to her after almost twenty years of dating and marriage. Just the solid wall of his arm in that dark suit, the touch of his mouth as he whispered to her, made her spin. She was so fortunate. The tears welled up again, and she grabbed another tissue from Laurel.

"We're a mess," her sister muttered. "A happy mess, but we are definitely a mess."

"It can only get better. I think they're almost to the end. At least we won't cry during the reception."

They didn't, because there was just too much going on all at once. The huge hall beneath the church was packed with people. Her father had insisted that they were not going to do a sit-down dinner and band and all the trimmings. "We know too many people who want to be here," he'd told the girls. "Nobody would have room to dance."

Claire had felt like arguing at the time, but her dad was right. The hall held several hundred people without a problem, and it was filled to capacity. Everybody in Friedens seemed to be here to wish Hank and Gloria well.

When Claire thought about it, that didn't surprise her. Gloria had been the leading Realtor in town about as long as her dad had been sheriff. Between them, it would be hard to find a family within twenty miles whose lives hadn't been touched by the people standing near the front table, smiling at each other.

Had she and Ben looked that happy nearly sixteen years ago? Of course they had, Claire told herself. But then, at the time she was all of eighteen, and Ben not quite twenty. They were too young and stupid to be anything but happy.

Not *stupid*, really, she mused. But they hadn't had any idea what they were up against—unlike Hank and Gloria, who'd been married before, raised children and each lost a spouse. Still, they looked radiant. Claire was filled with the impulse to go over and hug her dad, to tell him how happy he looked.

Not that he'd take well to a hug in public, even now. But she could get away with it here. As she crossed the floor toward Hank, she looked around to see where the boys had gotten to. Kyle must have seen her searching, because he bounded up to her.

At least he'd looked presentable during the wedding. The eleven-year-old was actually wearing a white shirt and tie, although the tie was drooping now and the top collar button was undone.

"Hey, Mom. You never told me Aunt Carrie could burp the alphabet."

Claire couldn't help shaking her head. "It just never occurred to me, Kyle. It's not a talent that gets much use, even for Carrie. Tell me she's not doing that for you guys here. Is she?''

''Not exactly. But she can spell words. Jeremy still has her beat on sound volume, anyway.''

There was that familiar dimple beside his grin. It looked just as appealing on her blond son as it did on her dark-haired husband.

''Which has more bubbles?'' he asked. ''Fountain soda or cans?''

''Cans. Don't shake them and don't join the contest, understood?'' She ran a hand through his hair, only to have him pull back.

''Gel, remember?''

Of course. Trent and Jeremy had helped him style the unruly mop before the wedding. ''Right. Sorry. And I mean it about being good, got it?''

''Got it,'' he said over his shoulder, heading over to join the beverage line and get his can of something extremely bubbly.

Maybe she should hunt down the boys and Carrie, and settle them down. Shaking her head again, Claire sought her father, instead.

''Sorry you didn't have a band?'' she asked him, giving him a quick hug. She was surprised when he answered her with a hearty squeeze right there in the middle of the church hall. If this was what marriage did for her usually reticent father, she liked it.

"A little bit. It would be fun dancing with Gloria. But then I'd get roped into dancing with all you girls, and two dozen ladies with blue hair, and I'm just as glad not to have to do that."

"I imagine." Claire looked over at Gloria, who had her granddaughter Mikayla on her hip and was straightening the stretchy headband in the child's fluffy pale hair. "So, are you two going to sneak out soon?"

Hank shrugged. "Don't see how we can for a while. I'm just glad we decided to go off to Branson for a few days. It will seem calm compared to this."

He put an arm around Claire again, and she marveled at the happiness in his blue eyes.

"Did I give you the last set of keys to the apartment?" he asked. "I can always come get them when we get back, to clear out the last of the boxes."

"You sure did. They're on the dresser, next to Ben's huge ring of keys from the hardware store. You could have kept a set if you wanted, though."

"It's safe this way. In more ways than one. This way if we have a spat, I don't have any way to go home to the family."

Claire giggled. "Right, Dad. That will happen. You two look like you couldn't be happier. And I'm sure it will last."

Hank winked at her. "If it lasts as long as you and Ben, we would make the papers as the oldest couple in the county, I think."

She thumped him on the shoulder, but gently. "I meant your happiness. And anyway, in sixteen years you'd only be—"

He put a finger to her lips. "Don't even go there, my dear. I know it's true, but I don't want to be reminded." Pulling back, he smiled, then came in to kiss her on the forehead in a very uncharacteristic, but endearing gesture. "I'll check in next week when we get back from Branson, and bring the truck over to move the last of the boxes. I'm down to odds and ends that Gloria doesn't want to see, I imagine."

"Like that elk head from Canada that Mom wouldn't let in the house, I'll bet."

Hank grinned. "You didn't notice that was already out of the garage? Gloria put it in the mudroom for a hat rack. The woman has quite a sense of humor."

"Yeah, she married you," Claire teased. "Seriously, though, all happiness. Have a good trip to Branson."

"We will. You two taking off now?"

Claire shook her head. "Not yet. And you know that by the time we leave it will be seven, not two. We've still got Laurel and Jeremy. And the boys, who are having some kind of contest with Carrie that I don't want to know about. I just wanted to come over here and catch you while I could.''

"Good job," Hank told her. "Of course you'd manage to come while Gloria was holding Mikayla. I'm sure that was pure coincidence.''

Gloria, hearing her name, came closer. "Coincidence, hmm? Where Claire and babies are concerned, I don't think so, Hank. I'd offer to let you hold her, but she's at that age where there aren't many people, besides her mom, that she'll go to.''

"She is a doll baby, though, isn't she?" Claire stroked the wispy hair, not getting close enough to frighten the wide-eyed child. "Like I told Dad, all the best. And have a great time in Branson.''

"I'm sure we will." Gloria's eyes glowed with happiness, and possibly with a few unshed tears.

Claire wondered what kind of feelings went through a woman's head on a second wedding day like this. It was hard for Claire to imagine.

Suddenly she had a question—for Ben. She knew it might be hours before she got her answer. But it was very important. She made her goodbyes, and found him discussing the fall football season and Friedens's chances against their biggest rival in Union.

Some of the folks in the discussion seemed to think Trent would automatically follow his father's lead as Friedens High School's star quarterback. Ben didn't disabuse them of the notion, even though he knew how Claire felt about the boys playing football. She was nervous enough that Trent would probably be on junior varsity in the fall.

When Ben slipped an arm around her, it was almost without looking—and, she suspected, without thinking. Just one of those automatic reactions because she was there.

The thought was still playing over in her mind later that same night, when she was standing at the bathroom mirror, brushing her hair before bed.

Sometimes it was very helpful to have your husband run a hardware store. Even if he didn't have the time to do all the work himself, they could afford all the materials to keep the place in shape. She was glad that they'd done the remodeling of the old house, giving them a real master bathroom. This way she could look in the mirror and through the doorway, if the door was open, see Ben in bed stretched out the way he was now, propped up on one elbow. How somebody looked that appealing in a plain gray T-shirt was beyond her.

"Ben? Wasn't it a nice wedding?" She put down the hairbrush and smoothed her shoulder-length waves. Still no gray among the light brown. Not everybody could say that at thirty-four.

"Nice? Sure. It was real nice." Ben seemed to be interested in the sports magazine on the bed.

"Can I ask you a question?"

"Any time." He still didn't lift his head from the magazine, but he was listening. That much she knew.

"I got the strangest feeling while I was at the reception watching Gloria and Dad. They looked so happy. Were we that happy?"

"Of course. We were so happy we nearly floated."

She could see his eyes in the mirror now, behind her, looking a little puzzled. "If you knew everything then, do you think you'd still do it the same way? Getting married that young, and all?" She wanted to add that *she* would—in a moment. But something stopped her. Perhaps it was the silence from the bedroom.

She could hear crickets outside through an open window. And little night-peeper frogs. But no answer from her husband. "Ben?" she asked again.

"I heard you. And honestly, I don't know."

As Claire turned toward the bed, it was as if the foundations of her world slipped slightly, pushing her off center.

Chapter Two

Claire sat on the side of the bed, wondering what to say. *What have I gotten myself into?* Was the question a prayer, or just an enquiry for her own spinning brain? She decided it had to be a prayer. She needed all the help she could get, because Ben's answer was not the one she expected.

"You want to explain that?" Her lips felt slightly numb as she spoke.

Ben looked down at his magazine, then flipped it closed and tossed it to the floor, backing up on the pillow to give her his full attention. She wasn't sure whether to be gratified or disturbed by the change.

"I know the safe answer would have been better, Claire. But it wouldn't have been the truth.

And we've always told each other the truth." Ben's blue eyes were frank. That was Ben. He didn't ever pull his punches.

"If my answer upsets you, it must be because yours is different. Does this mean that you'd do it all again, the same way we did it, without any questions? Even if you knew everything you know now?"

"Ten minutes ago I would have said yes. Of course." Claire noticed that her feet were cold. And her fingers were, too. She pulled up into a ball on the bed, tucking her toes under the hem of her cotton gown. She must have shivered, because Ben pulled her close.

She felt as if she should pull away, given their discussion. Her husband had just told her that he might not marry her again at nineteen if he had the wisdom of a thirty-five-year-old. But still, this was *Ben.* He had been part of her life forever, or at least since she was barely fourteen, younger than Trent. "How can you say no?" she asked through lips that were still numb.

He pulled her even closer, and Claire snuggled in to his body. She felt traitorous for seeking comfort from the very man who had upset her, but there could be no one else for her in any situation. "I didn't. You asked if I'd do it again. And I told you the truth. I don't know." He rested his head back on the headboard.

"Why don't you know?" Claire wasn't so sure she wanted to find out, but she had to ask.

"Don't you ever wonder?" His voice sounded almost harsh. "What if we'd waited? What if you'd finished college instead of marrying me and having Trent so quickly? Would we still be here, living in your parents' old house, in the town we both grew up in? I know I would have kept playing college ball. Maybe even gone pro instead of coming back here to run Dad's hardware store. Don't you ever think that maybe we could have done better?"

Claire buried her face in his neck, feeling his arm around her, knowing she could never have done any better than this. How did she tell him that, and still answer his question honestly? They were talking about two different things.

She was asking if he loved her in the same way, if he would go through all the thrills and storms of marriage again, knowing now what no nineteen-year-old could know. He was answering with a practical thought about the rest of their life choices.

To Claire, it was apples and oranges. To Ben, it was more like Golden Delicious versus Granny Smith.

"Claire? Now I've got to ask. You still there?

It never takes *you* this long to answer." He sounded amused and worried at the same time.

"I'm here. And thinking. Maybe if you put it like that, I'd have to answer the same way. Sure, I wonder what things would have been like if we'd waited. But I can't imagine life without Trent and Kyle."

"I can. We could afford vacations, have shrimp for dinner instead of hamburger, and I'd drive a convertible—"

Even without looking Claire could tell that her husband was grinning as he spoke. It made her want to poke him in the rib cage.

"But I'd probably hate every minute of it."

Relief washed over Claire like a wave. "You had me worried for a minute."

"Sorry. I didn't intend to." He kissed her softly, first at the hairline and then on the lips, gently. "You know I don't like worrying you. You worry too much as it is."

"Who, me?" Claire batted her eyelashes at him, watching him smile.

"You're the queen of worriers." But the words were teasing and familiar, making Claire smile.

She didn't feel cold anymore. But she was getting sleepy. "Want to turn out the light?"

Ben's answer was to reach his free arm over to the nightstand and find the lamp. In a moment they were in the dark, with only the crickets and peepers for company.

Did those stupid frogs ever shut up? Ben lay awake in the dark, listening to them. Every spring Claire could hardly wait to open the windows in the bedroom while they slept. For him, it was four to six weeks of aggravation. When the pollen wasn't killing him, the frogs were keeping him up. Still, Ben didn't have the heart to ask her to sleep with the windows shut all year round. He got his way most of the time. What were a couple of nights of rocky sleep?

Besides, if he were truly honest with himself, it wasn't the frogs that were keeping him up tonight. It was Claire's question, and the look on her face when he answered. For a minute there, he thought she was going to lose it.

This was one of those times when a polite lie would have been better than the truth. But polite lies had never been what he and Claire told each other. Not for things that really counted.

Of course, there were his business worries. But the store was his problem. Definitely not something he needed to share with his wife. A good accountant, maybe. But the conversation they had just had was something different.

Running it through his mind, he was still confused. Even his more complex answer wasn't what Claire had wanted. What was she really asking, anyway? It was harder to figure out his beautiful wife than to figure out some of his customers at the store—even the ones who came in with half a part missing from something, having no idea what they were looking for.

She had looked so beautiful today. He'd been struck in the church hall, watching her talk to Hank and Gloria, how little she'd changed in twenty years. If he closed his eyes a little he could imagine that the woman across the hall was wearing white satin and his freshly bought ring.

Now *there* was one of the things he'd do differently if he could. He would have bought Claire a diamond to go with that skinny little gold band. Not that there had been many times when he could have afforded a diamond. Certainly none in the first ten years they were married. And not really now, either.

But she deserved the diamond. That was the kind of thing he was talking about. And if they'd waited to get married, would he really be running the store now? Yeah, probably by now. Thirty-five was ancient in pro football. But surely he would have gotten his chance for a couple of years. Between college and running the store there might have been somebody willing to pay the big bucks.

Claire could have her diamond. There'd be college savings accounts for the boys. Maybe even a new house in one of those subdivisions outside town where the doctors and lawyers all lived, instead of her parents' house, which was older than him or Claire. Who could say?

So many facets of life might be different if he hadn't talked Claire into getting married when they were both still teenagers. And how many things would be different if he hadn't been somebody's daddy before his twenty-first birthday? Not that he had anybody to blame for that but himself. Trent had been as big a surprise to Claire as he had been to Ben. They both adored him, and Kyle, too. The boys were great. Still, Ben had to wonder what life would be like without kids, or at least without kids so early.

Claire slept peacefully beside him. He listened to her even breathing, felt the soft exhalations near his arm. She was so sweet, so lovely that it didn't seem like twenty years could have passed since their first date in high school. Wasn't she still a freshman?

Ben shook his head. No, afraid not. Their oldest son had just finished freshman year. And Ben himself was the guy responsible for putting food on the table to feed two growing boys, and keeping a roof over their heads. No time to lose sleep over daydreams of what might have been.

For a change he decided to really listen to the dumb peeper frogs. Maybe if he listened long enough, they'd bore him to sleep. This late at night, anything was worth a try.

The next morning Claire had to face the fact that her sister was going home to California. "Are you sure you have to go back so soon?" Laurel didn't look happy about her decision, either. To Claire, Laurel seemed close to tears as she picked up the last suitcase.

"I don't want to. When we made the reservations it made perfect sense to just come for the long weekend and then go back there," Laurel said. "I'd forgotten how different it is here."

"It has to be a change from California."

Laurel nodded. "In so many ways. When Sam was around it made sense to stay there. I mean, where else does a screenwriter make a living? But now that he's gone, it just doesn't make as much sense."

"You'd have a revolt on your hands if you tried to move back here, though, wouldn't you?" They looked out to the broad asphalt driveway between the garage and apartment and the main house. Laurel's gangly son Jeremy was showing his cousins another trick on his skateboard, while Trent and Kyle had their in-line skates on and the hockey equipment out. Neither side appeared to convince the other that their way was better, but both were having fun.

Each taking a suitcase, the women went down the stairs. They put the baggage on the pavement for the kids to load into the car in a few minutes when Ben came back. "You know it. Jer is a California kid. He can't imagine anyplace else. But I worry about the influences out there, and the schools and everything. I miss my family, and I guess I'm just too practical for California."

"How's that?" Claire asked, still watching the boys banter on the driveway.

"We could probably get by on about a third of what we do out there, if we moved back to Missouri. Not that Sam left me hurting for money, but I want to keep everything I can in savings to send Jeremy to college."

"I hear you. It's scary to think they're that close to going, isn't it?"

"Not that Jeremy appreciates the idea." Claire could hear the aggravation thick in her sister's voice. "He says he doesn't need to go to college to be a pro skateboarder, which is what he wants to do."

"But think of how much money it would save

you. Surely, that's what he's thinking of, isn't it? Trent hasn't even tried the 'I don't need college' argument. He knows that Ben and I are both determined that he's going to start—and finish. There's going to be at least one Jericho with a four-year degree around here.''

Claire felt her sister's hand on her shoulder. ''I always thought that you would be first.''

She looked at Laurel. Her sister wasn't teasing. ''Really? What would I do?''

''I don't know. Art. Fashion design. Something using all those creative talents. You always did better in school than I did, Claire. It didn't bother Mom and Dad as much when I dropped out after one year of college. But when you and Ben insisted you were getting married right away, and he was the only one going back to school, I thought Daddy would explode.''

Claire shrugged. ''He survived. And so did I. And it really was for the best, anyway. What would I do with a degree?''

''Something. You've still got the same wonderful talent and creativity. It shows up in almost everything you touch, whether it's painting the bathroom or putting together an outfit for Dad's wedding. And it's certainly wasted on your family.''

Claire bristled and started to argue. Then she

closed her mouth. No sense getting into an argument with Laurel when they only had moments before driving to the airport. Especially when her sister was more than half-right. She was aggravating as only a big sister could be, but on track.

"Okay, I'll give you that one. And I am about ready to do something different. What about you?"

Claire turned to her sister, surprised to see her eyes glittering with unshed tears. She hadn't realized that Laurel was that serious about things. "Hey, we'll both be okay," she said, gathering her for a hug.

"I know," Laurel said shakily, returning the hug. She pulled away, wiping one escaping tear off her cheek. "It's just that everything is so hard sometimes. And I know what I want to do, but not whether I can do it."

She looked back at the apartment. "Just don't rent that out right away, will you?"

"I hadn't planned to. Do you really think you could move back here?" The thought of having both her sisters close enough to visit with on a regular basis was a new and heady thing.

Laurel nodded. "I'm praying for change. And you know how dangerous that is." Her use of one of their mother's favorite phrases from their childhood made Claire smile. Ever the optimist, Susan

Collins had told her daughters to pray for change, and then count on God to make it happen.

"But expect to be surprised." Claire could hear her mother's rich voice. *"Because the Lord's idea of change and ours isn't always the same."* It hadn't been in her mom's case, that was for certain. Still, through six years of struggle with cancer and remission, and ultimately more cancer, Sue had found healing. It had always been there for her spirit, if not for her body in the end.

"Pray for some of that change for me while you're at it." Where had those words come from? Claire had surprised herself. Wasn't she perfectly content with her life just the way it was?

No, she wasn't. Her life was wonderful and fulfilling, but it was time for a change. Even in the warm June sunshine, the thought made her shiver.

Laurel saw her shudder, and put an arm around her again. It felt so good to have her comforting, annoying older sister this close. Maybe it would be a good idea to have her around all the time.

"We'll pray for each other," said Laurel. "For the most wonderful and dangerous changes we can think of. Now where is that husband of yours? It's an hour drive at least to the airport."

"Forty-five minutes," Claire countered. "You forget how he drives. Still, I better go in and call."

Claire went into the kitchen and punched in the

familiar number. "Jericho Hardware," said a friendly voice. It wasn't Ben, which gave her hope.

"Hi, Pete. Great. Tell me you answering the phone means that Ben is on his way back here to get to the airport."

"Uh, not exactly, Mrs. Jericho."

Claire could feel her spirits fall. Not again. The young clerk sounded like he had bad news, or at least news he was reluctant to break himself.

"Do you want to talk to him?"

"Yes, please," she said through tight lips. Pete put her on hold for a while. About the time she was ready to hang up, Ben finally came on the line.

"Hi. I'm not there, obviously. Something came up."

It was all Claire could do to keep herself from scowling or saying something rude. If this weren't a normal occurrence, she'd be pleasant. But it happened far too often lately. "Oh? Ben, you knew when you left this morning that you were supposed to be coming back to take Laurel and Jeremy."

He sighed. "I know. But the person I'd set up an important appointment with, for tomorrow, just breezed in the door ten minutes ago. Apparently we got our days mixed up."

"Can't you just—" Claire started.

"No. I can't do anything right now but stay here

and be cordial." Ben wasn't leaving any room for argument or compromise.

That surprised her. Usually when this happened he tried to find some way to placate her. Not this time.

He went on, still sounding just as firm. "This is too important to do anything else. I'm sorry. I'll make it up to you, I promise. Tell Laurel and Jer goodbye for me, okay?"

"Sure." Claire hung up the phone and looked around the room for her keys to the truck. Great. It probably didn't even have gas in it—not enough to get to St. Louis, anyway. At least it wasn't rush hour.

"Looks like we're on our own," she told her sister.

Laurel made a face. "Lovely. Just promise me I won't be explaining anything to the highway patrol. Although, I expect we could get Carrie to fix any ticket you got."

"Not this month. I've already made my quota." It was worth the teasing just to see the look on her sister's face. Claire wondered what Laurel would say if she knew that her teasing had an edge of truth. She promised herself to watch the speed all the way to the airport. At least the boys were staying home, so there wouldn't be anybody along to rat her out.

She called them to the truck to load the suitcases. If she was surrounded by big hulking males, might as well put those strong bodies to good use. No need to do everything herself, even if Ben was leaving her in the lurch. *Again,* a voice in her mind told her.

"Definitely pray for some change around here," she told Laurel. "It's about time."

Chapter Three

Claire was almost glad Ben didn't come home in time for supper that night. The dinner table was no place to argue. And she knew that given the chance tonight, she'd argue. It was easier to put together sub sandwiches and get the guys fed early, then get them to their respective activities.

Kyle was getting ready for Scout camp. He was old enough now that he went to Boy Scout camp without a parent, and he was excited about it. Claire was thankful that he'd reached the age of going with the Boy Scouts instead of the Cubs, because there was no way Ben's schedule could have accommodated a week of camping. When had they all gotten so busy?

Trent was just going over to a friend's house

with his street hockey equipment for a quick game. It stayed light so long at this time of year, they could play for hours. Once both boys were dropped off, Claire could escape to the relative peace of her women's fellowship at church. When Ben came home he'd find her note telling him where everybody was, and a sandwich in the refrigerator, so everything was taken care of.

After a weekend of activity, and seeing so much of her sisters, it was fun to be in the company of her church friends again. Many of them had been at her dad's wedding, and had some comment about the flowers or the music. It was nice to remember her happy weekend instead of her aggravating day.

Finally Debi Baker, the head of the fellowship group, got everyone to settle down so she could get the evening's program started. The woman she introduced looked so polished and put together that Claire felt a twinge of envy.

Granted, anybody presenting a program to a group wanted to look her best. But how long had it been since Claire had come to fellowship in something other than a denim skirt, or maybe a pair of khakis and a cotton shirt, if she'd gotten to the ironing? Her household priorities, and picking up the slack for Ben as often as not, made her own appearance last on the list quite often. This woman looked as if she'd just stepped out of a corporate meeting.

Debi introduced her, and the woman smiled at their welcoming applause. "Thank you. I feel like part of the group already. And that's good, because I want to lay something on your hearts this evening. It's June. Traditionally the season for graduations. And weddings. Who could tell me what they were doing in June, say, four or five years ago?"

A few hands went up. Claire could have told the lovely speaker what she was doing any June in the last fifteen years. And none of it involved the kind of glamour she was sure that this young woman had seen in life.

"As Ms. Baker told you before, I'm Nessa Hart, and I'm the regional director of The Caring Closet. And five years ago this June, I was a single mom with two small children, collecting public assistance while watching them grow up in a St. Louis housing project."

There was a murmur through the group. Claire found herself backing up in her chair. This woman? Collecting welfare? It didn't add up with her polished appearance and self-confidence. When Nessa Hart began to explain how the changes in her life had come about in five years, Claire felt a thrill go through her. Talk about dramatic change.

"Once I knew Jesus, my whole life changed. But it was harder to match the changes on the inside with changes on the outside, where people could see them," Nessa told them. "I could change my life and become a different person. But that person needed schooling to do a job, and clothes to go to interviews and get that job. That's where The Caring Closet came in. Obviously, I'm a believer in what they do." Nessa was smiling as she spoke. "I passed up a promotion at another job to come and work for them. And I've never had any doubts that this was the right decision for me. It was the only thing I could do to give back, to launch somebody else on the same path I followed."

While Nessa went on explaining The Caring Closet's mission in outfitting women for the work world, a persistent thought began whispering over and over through Claire's mind. *You could do this. You could really do this.* It wasn't the sort of thing she had had in mind when she asked Laurel to pray for change. But maybe it was even better. She could hardly wait to get home and talk to Ben. She didn't even stay for cookies after fellowship—and they were chocolate chip with pecans, her favorite.

Every light was on in the house when she got to the driveway. Ben's car was parked, and Claire could hear the commotion of the guys in the kitchen as she got out of the truck and headed for the back door.

Trent's hockey equipment nearly tripped her just inside. Kyle was digging into the closet in the mudroom, holding a piece of pizza in one hand. "Hi, Mom," she heard him say from halfway in the closet. "Do you know where the rest of the tent stakes are?"

"Should be in a zipper pouch with the tent, Kyle. And either look for tent stakes or eat pizza, but not both at the same time."

"Okay." The hand holding the pizza disappeared inside the closet with the rest of Kyle. That wasn't exactly what she'd meant, but Claire decided to let it slide for now. She was so anxious to talk to Ben, she'd even let Kyle eat in the closet.

As she looked into the kitchen for him, an explosion rumbled from the table. It was the kind of noise that could only come from the gullet of a well-stuffed human male loaded with pizza and cola. "Ugh. What do you say, Trent?" she prompted.

"Nice resonance, Dad." Her son's reply brought Claire's head up quickly.

"Benjamin Trent Jericho, you didn't do that— did you?" His grin was all the answer she needed. "That's terrible. What are you teaching these guys?"

"Nothing. At least, not on purpose. I've been on my feet for a good solid twelve hours, and I guess I ate dinner too fast. Sorry."

Ben was pushed back from the kitchen table, tie loosened and shoes kicked off. His face showed signs of fatigue behind the grin. Claire came up behind him, not sure whether to stroke his dark hair or yank it out by the roots. The softness beneath her fingers convinced her not to pull.

"Okay, I guess I'll let you off this once. But you didn't have to bring home pizza. There was dinner in the refrigerator."

Ben looked up into her face, seeming surprised. The motion pushed his head into her midsection, almost making her forget the exciting things she wanted to tell him about her fellowship meeting.

"Wow. You must want something. You don't usually let me get away with anything that easy." He quirked one eyebrow, questioning her.

The man knew her way too well. That was one of the downsides of marrying your high school sweetheart. Things got very predictable at times. "Maybe. Well, okay, yes. I do want something. Let me tell you about what I found out tonight."

Ben held up a hand. "If it's church gossip, I don't want to know."

Claire resisted the urge to really yank that beautiful wavy dark mane. "You know better than that.

Do you want more of that soda to drink while you listen to this?''

Ben sighed. "Sure. But if you pour some for yourself, make it decaffeinated. You seem to have enough charge already this evening.''

Ben sat at the kitchen table, trying very hard to focus on what Claire was saying. It wasn't easy. There was already so much other stuff bouncing around in his brain. And her enthusiasm made her glow. Both those things together made him want to scoop her up and take her upstairs, instead of having a serious discussion.

Claire really wanted this discussion, though, so he was going to have to put his thoughts on hold and pay attention. It was still hard for him to follow her train of thought.

"Now let me get this straight," he said, when she paused for a moment. "This is something you really want to do on your own?'' It just didn't sound like Claire.

Claire nodded. "It really is. The women's fellowship group is really excited about starting this community closet idea. And I could do it.''

"Sounds to me like a giant rummage sale with no profit.'' At least it wasn't going to cost him anything. Although knowing Claire, she'd find a way to make it cost him something.

Claire's brow wrinkled. "Then you're missing the point, or I'm not explaining things very clearly."

"Must be me. We know you're always crystal clear in your explanations." That would probably get a coaster tossed at his head, but he couldn't resist.

"Very funny. Let me try it again. Maybe I should start by asking what you don't understand."

"Why anybody would want to spend weeks, or maybe even months, sorting through a bunch of cast-off clothing, if you're not going to either bale it up and send it someplace to a mission, or sell it to make a profit."

Claire took a deep breath. "Okay. I'll try to give you the short story that Nessa gave us. I did tell you about Nessa, didn't I?"

Now it was Ben's turn to nod. "And she must have really impressed you."

"She did. And what she said was so simple, Ben. See, this program gathers good, gently used women's business apparel. Then it recycles the clothing to people who need to go on job interviews, start an office job, whatever."

Her eyes widened into dark pools again, bringing back Ben's urge to hold her.

"Imagine it. You gather the skills to get your family off public assistance and finally be self-supporting. But when you go out to do interviews, nobody hires you because you don't have a suit or nice shoes or a briefcase to carry your papers in." Her eyes blazed. "Ben, that's just not fair."

"Of course it isn't. Life in general doesn't seem to be most of the time." If Claire hadn't figured that out by now, he must have been sheltering her even more than he thought.

"I know. But most things that aren't fair, I can't do much about. This I can."

Claire pulled her long legs up in the chair with her, wrapping her arms around them. Then she started ticking off reasons on her fingers, while Ben tried to listen instead of just watching the dancing fingertips.

"I know how to organize things. I know who to get hold of to get the church a quality supply of gently used business clothes. And they've already got most of the space in the Sunday School building, so I wouldn't even have to take up much room here."

"Much room? We don't have *any* room to run a thrift shop out of the house."

There was that forehead wrinkle again.

"It's not a thrift shop. I keep trying to tell you that. It's a community service. And we wouldn't do anything but sort a few things here, anyway."

Ah, Claire and her enthusiasm. "Please, define

a few of those terms. Like who 'we' would be, and what kind of 'few things' you would be sorting, whoever you are."

She sighed. It was really more of a snort of impatience, but if he pointed that out she'd offer to deck him. Claire saw herself as more genteel than sixteen years of life with the guys had made her.

"I don't know who everybody will be yet. Whoever else decides that this is the project of their hearts, I guess. And we'd sort things here until we got them in some sort of shape to take to church. And when I say here, I really mean Dad's apartment. It's vacant, and nobody needs it for anything."

"So nice of you to consult me before deciding that." Now Ben knew he was the one who sounded sharp.

"Well? Do you need it for anything?" Claire challenged.

"I might." That sounded like the boys arguing. Maybe even less mature. "I guess it would have been nice to be asked before you made up your mind on all this. You didn't tell them at church that you'd do it, did you?"

There was that snort again.

"I most certainly did not. Am I usually that impulsive?"

Ben shrugged. "Where good works are concerned, I have to say yes, sometimes you are."

"Not on anything this big. This is a project that won't be over in six weeks. Just setting it up will take that long or longer. And then whoever commits to leading the group will probably have to commit a year or more to the leadership."

Ben whistled. "A year? As in twelve months, volunteer, just out of the goodness of your heart?"

"A year. Not full time or anything. Some weeks it would be only a few hours, some more like fifteen or twenty, depending on what stage of things we're in. And yes, it would be all volunteer. This is a service, a ministry." Her brow wrinkled again. "Besides, it's not like anybody's paying me now to do anything."

"That's true. But I thought that was the way you wanted things. The way we both wanted things." This conversation was changing his whole opinion of his wife.

"It was. And it still is, for the most part. But I believe I can do this. More than that, I *want* to do this. It sounds like a really good fit for me. I just told Laurel to pray for change. I'm ready for a little change in my life."

Great. So now this crazy scheme was the answer to a prayer. "So now if I protest I'm keeping you from doing what God wants you to."

Claire bristled. "I didn't say that. Is there something else you'd rather see me doing?" She looked so determined. And so appealing, eyes sparkling, lips in a decisive pout.

"Not really. It just seems like they're taking advantage of your good nature in a big way. I mean, I wouldn't volunteer to take on a project like this for anything. It would be stupid."

Her mouth compressed. "Well, maybe that's just the difference between us, then. I won't make a decision tonight, anyway. I need to think on it, pray on it."

"And sleep on it?" Ben tried not to sound suggestive. Claire knew how he felt, anyway. He was as hopeless in his admiration of her as he had been fifteen years ago. Why was he arguing against this crazy scheme? It would probably keep her from being interested in any changes he made at work in the near future. And that would be a very good thing.

"And sleep on it." Funny, it sounded different when she said it. Like she actually intended to sleep. Ben tried not to sigh or look too wishful. That would just get her more stirred up than she already was.

On Wednesday morning Claire was still thinking and planning. She hadn't given anybody an answer at church on whether she'd take over The Caring Closet, but she was pretty sure she would. It sounded like a lot of work, but interesting work.

In the long run it would be a project that helped so many people. Women who needed a way to improve their lives, and the lives of their children, would get help in a positive, encouraging way. And at the same time, a lot of people who had closets full of clothes they weren't using could feel good about clearing those things out.

Claire thought about her own closet. There were several outfits that would be going to this ministry, whether she headed it up or not. That blue blazer she hadn't worn since she stopped being president of the PTA. And there was that wool dress with the pleated skirt. Ben liked it on her, but she always felt like it made her hips look too wide. Besides, it was wool and it itched. She always felt like fidgeting or running her finger around the inside of her collar about halfway through Sunday School. Since she was always admonishing the boys not to wiggle, she couldn't very well do the same thing.

She decided to get two things done at once: go through the closets for discards for church, and get a load of laundry done.

She thought best while doing things like that, anyway. Those dozens of little mindless tasks that had to be done around the house kept her hands busy, but not her mind. She could weigh the decision in front of her while she sorted laundry and matched socks.

Her side of the closet was easy. None of her dirty clothes ever got waylaid on the way to the hamper. She found the two things she wanted to set aside and laid them on the bed, then looked around the room.

There weren't many of Ben's clothes strewn around, for a change. If she had a nickel for every stray sock she'd picked up in sixteen years, she could probably buy a new washer. One pair of khakis was draped over the chair where he'd left them. Claire picked up the pants, looking them over for odd stains or rips. Ben was as hard on his clothes as were the boys.

The khakis seemed to be in one piece, and there were no obvious ugly stains like machine oil or paint or the other stuff he got into at the hardware store and then forgot to tell her about. Washing clothes was often an adventure around here.

As she put the pants over her arm to take to the basket in the hallway, Claire heard a rustle. She reached into the front pockets, checking for whatever Ben had left in there. There was a piece of paper, folded in quarters. It was nice business letterhead. There was a matching business card folded into the paper. Claire read it, wondering what it was all about. Going to the nightstand, she dialed the phone. Surprisingly enough, Ben answered himself.

"Hey. It's me." She balanced the phone between her shoulder and ear. "I'm doing laundry, and I found some papers in your pocket. Who's Marcy McKinnon?"

"You remember her. From high school. Except she was Marcy Farley then."

"Oh." Marcy Farley McKinnon had been the prettiest blond cheerleader at Friedens High when Ben was a senior. She was the one people had always said Ben should have been dating instead of mousy, scholarly sophomore Claire Collins. Even Claire knew folks said that behind her back.

"Has she moved back to town, then?"

"No, still living in St. Louis. But she was my business appointment the other morning, when you ended up taking Laurel and Jeremy to the airport."

"Oh." She sounded like a broken record, but she felt stunned. "What kind of business were you discussing with Marcy McKinnon?"

There was a long pause on Ben's end of the line. She could hear somebody ringing up a sale on the cash register, then the rattle of plastic bags as a purchase was handed over. It seemed like forever, and he still hadn't answered.

Finally he cleared his throat. It was still a moment before he spoke. "I can't tell you what I was discussing with her."

"Not at all?"

She could almost feel him shaking his head in that slow, solid way he had.

"Not at all. Just put the papers on my desk in the living room, okay?"

Like a good little wife, his tone seemed to say. "I guess. Does this mean we'll discuss this when you get home?"

She could tell that he was trying to sound light, but his voice sounded strained. "Afraid not. This isn't something I can discuss with you. Not for the present, at least. But it isn't anything to worry about. I'll see you at dinner."

With that the phone went dead. And Claire was standing in the middle of the bedroom holding a strange woman's business card and feeling more confused than she had in years.

Chapter Four

Dinner that night was a strange event. It was a night on which everyone was home, which was usually cause for celebration. With Ben as busy as he was, and the kids constantly involved in activities after school, with friends or with their youth groups at church, it was rare that everyone was at the table together on a weeknight.

Claire knew it was mostly her own attitude that kept things from being party-like. She felt tense and brittle enough to break. Meanwhile, Ben sat at the table calmly. He seemed totally unaware that he'd upset her.

The boys seemed to sense the tense atmosphere, and concentrated on eating instead of talking. Dishes on the table emptied at a surprising rate.

Finally in the silence, broken before only by the *clink* of cutlery, Kyle cleared his throat.

"Uh, Mom? I heard you talking about that closet thing at church. Are you going to do it?"

"I don't know yet. Probably. Why?"

Kyle shrugged. His shoulders were thinner, but the gesture looked so much like one of Ben's.

"It sounds like a lot of work, is all. Don't you have enough to do already?"

Claire wanted to shout her answer, but this was her sweet baby asking. He needed gentle education, even though she was feeling aggravation and frustration. "Most of the things I do, anybody could do around here. Cooking and cleaning and laundry aren't just 'Mom stuff' as much as they are survival skills. And it's probably time you guys knew a whole bunch more about them."

Kyle groaned. "Now you sound like Aunt Laurel. Do you know that Jeremy does all his own laundry? He doesn't do any cleaning, though."

"Yeah, well, that's because his mom doesn't, either, doofus," Trent chimed in. "They have somebody come in and clean. That's how it's done when you're rich."

Claire's frustration was growing with the realization of her children's attitudes. She breathed a silent prayer for help before going on. "I don't ever remember saying that Aunt Laurel and Jeremy are rich. Or that what your cousin does or doesn't do will matter in your chores—and don't call your brother names.''

Trent glared at his brother, as if it were his fault somehow that Claire had corrected them both. He knew better than to say anything out loud. That was one area of discipline on which both his parents, even if they weren't speaking much to each other, agreed.

Kyle seemed oblivious to any correction aimed at him. ''Hey, does this mean Dad has to pitch in more on chores too, if we do?''

Trent snickered. ''Sure. He can cook if Mom gets stuck at church doing the closet thing.''

Claire tried not to laugh. She wondered if Ben knew enough about cooking to get past boiling water or making toast. Everything would definitely be grilled if he cooked. ''I'm sure we could find something for him to do. Cooking might not be the right thing.''

''Good. I'm too young to die.''

Kyle's grin was a version of his father's. And his reflexes were almost as good as his father's, allowing him to duck quickly when Ben swiped a hand at his head in mock anger.

''Thanks, pal. I'll remember you the next time I'm making burgers. One charred one coming up.''

''Great. And I can't even feed it to the dog, because Mom won't let us have one. I'll bet we never get a dog if you do this closet thing at church.''

Trent looked honestly worried for a moment. ''You'll still do band boosters at school, won't you? And drive me to hockey at Jeff's?''

''I might not be available every moment,'' Claire admitted. ''But you guys know you won't actually suffer from my taking on a project at church.''

''We'll suffer if you make Dad cook,'' Kyle muttered. ''Can I be excused?''

Claire shook her head. ''Go. Just remember to clear your dishes and stack them by the sink.''

He slid out of his seat and did what he was told. Trent followed, leaving the kitchen to the adults. Claire waited for a few minutes, wondering if Ben would bring up the cause of the silence between them.

He moved things around on his plate a little, staying quiet. Apparently he'd decided that the best way to avoid an argument was to say nothing.

Sometimes that worked. But tonight Claire couldn't stand the silence for long. ''I put those papers on top of your dresser. Did you find them?''

''Yes, I did. Thanks.''

Great. She was getting the condensed version. This wasn't going to be easy. ''Does this mean you still aren't going to explain what you're doing seeing Marcy McKinnon?"

Ben looked up, his brows pulled together in aggravation. "I am not 'seeing' Marcy. You make things sound so out of line. All the woman did was stop by for a business appointment."

"Which you won't explain to me," Claire pointed out.

"Normally, you want me to leave the business at the front door when I come home."

How could he be so perfectly reasonable when he knew it was only going to annoy her more? "'Normally' doesn't include business appointments with the girl the whole high school paired you up with all of your senior year."

Claire was immediately aware how juvenile that sounded. But it had disturbed her. How had their lives gotten so out of whack that Ben didn't tell her something like this?

Ben's expression was odd, almost bemused. "Did they really? That's funny." He straightened in his chair. "It's also beside the point. Marcy was at the store on business. And it's not business I can discuss right now without jeopardizing a deal that could mean something to us. It's not like you're normally involved in my business decisions, Claire."

She couldn't stand sitting at the table anymore.

Claire pushed away and picked up an armload of dishes. She concentrated on setting things down on the countertop without banging them. No sense chipping the china just because she was mad at Ben.

"That's what I'm getting at. I should be involved in those decisions, don't you think? Just yesterday you got on me for not consulting you before I made a decision. And I hadn't even made one yet."

Ben was up now, following her to the sink. He put his hands on her shoulders, and Claire resisted the urge to shrug him off. She didn't want to push him any farther away than he already was. She must have stiffened under his touch, because in a moment he let go on his own.

"Maybe you're right. Maybe it's time for more of a partnership in the business. But Claire, that's not what I'm used to. Our partnership has always been me at the store, you at home."

Claire's anger flared. "Only because we drifted into things that way. I didn't finish college and get a business degree or anything that would help you. I had Trent instead, remember? And then Kyle came along, and there was always plenty to do here. Because we both wanted me staying home with them. Or, at least, that's the way I understood things."

He was still behind her. Claire could feel his warm breath near the back of her neck, and for a moment she wanted to lean into his comforting warmth. Ben was her rock, even when they didn't get along. Fighting with him was never pleasant.

"That's the way things were. But I just figured it was the way they still would be. Are you telling me you're unhappy? That you want a change?"

"Maybe." Claire stepped away, where his warm breath wouldn't confuse her thoughts. "I guess I want to change the partnership a little. Diversify."

She turned around and leaned against the sink. That could be a mistake, looking into Ben's warm, dark eyes. If she weren't careful, this argument would end the way of all their arguments, with him promising plenty, changing nothing and romancing her into complacency.

Except that when she turned around, the look on Ben's face assured that she wasn't going to be romanced into anything tonight. "I could just smack you, Ben Jericho. You've got that 'isn't she cute for using the big business word' smirk on your face."

Ben's grin faded. "I didn't mean to. But I can't help thinking you might be a little out of your league with all this. Which is the major reason I can't explain what I'm discussing with Marcy. And the major reason I'd like you to think about what

Kyle calls 'the closet thing.'" He reached out toward her, and Claire scooted away.

"I look at you, and I still see the sweet thing I married. And I promised to honor you, protect you, cherish you."

Now that sounded like a caveman. "Yeah, but you didn't promise to treat me like a child or an idiot. And we're both different from those two kids who got married back in the Dark Ages."

"Not so different," Ben began, heading toward her with his usual argument-winning tactics.

This time it wasn't going to work. "Not tonight, Ben." She planted a hand firmly on his chest. He seemed surprised that she would actually resist his charms. "Tonight I need to make it very clear to you that your sweet young thing is all grown up. And she's got a lot more sense than you give her credit for."

His brows pulled together again, and Ben moved half a step back. Her hand stayed on his chest, holding him at bay. It was difficult, but she was determined.

"I'll give you a lot of credit, Claire. Running the house and raising the boys takes effort. But I still don't think you're up to business responsibilities at Jericho Hardware or running a huge mission project at church. Just as I don't think I could do your job here."

Now her anger really blazed. Claire drew back, planted one fist on her hip and shook the other at him in anger. "Is that what you see all this as? My *job?* Well, I've got news for you, housework and raising children are a lot more challenging than you think. And I'm more than half tempted to see if you could do 'my job,' just to show you how much you don't know."

Ben's eyes sparked. "Is that a dare? Because if it is..."

The back of her neck prickled. "I think it is. Yes, that's a dare. A double-dog dare like Harley Fox gave you to climb the flagpole during your senior year. I dare you to try my job for a month, Ben. And I bet you anything you like that you'll be less successful at it than I will be at running The Caring Closet."

"Anything I like? You're on." He moved in on her. Claire found herself no place to go to escape, having backed herself into a corner of the kitchen already. "And there's only one way to seal this kind of double-dog dare bet."

He leaned down and captured her lips before she could protest. Opening her mouth to argue would only intensity the kiss that Ben was giving her. Claire found her fingers twined in his rumpled dark hair.

Finally he broke the kiss and looked down at

her. It took a moment for her to clear her head and gather enough air to speak. "Double-dog dare or not, I know you didn't kiss Harley Fox," she said.

"He wasn't nearly as cute as you, even when you're riled up." With a wink and a grin, Ben walked out of the kitchen, leaving her to fume in silence at the outcome of another argument. Even though she'd gotten what she wanted, it still felt as if he'd won. It always felt like he won. How did he do that?

He was an idiot. A purebred fool. How could he have gotten himself into this much trouble all at once? Ben sat in his recliner, behind the newspaper, not really reading it, not paying any attention to the baseball game on television, either. He was using both as distractions from his problems. Neither was working.

Why didn't he just go back into the kitchen and confess everything to Claire? That he was a miserable failure and he'd finally gotten to the point where talking to an outside business broker about selling the family business was the only option. That the broker happened to be Marcy McKinnon, whom he barely remembered from high school, struck him as a huge coincidence. That obviously was not the way Claire would see it.

From Claire's perspective, he seemed to be planning something shady with another woman. That was the last thing on his mind. He couldn't imagine anything he'd ever done that would give Claire any ideas in that direction.

Still, at this point he'd rather have Claire thinking that he might be flirting with another woman. It beat having her know that her husband was such a loser. Not that everything facing him was his fault. In fact, most of it was totally out of his control, which is what made him so mad.

The big discount and chain stores out on the highway took most of the hardware business these days. There was no way a little mom-and-pop like Jericho could match their prices on everyday stuff like tools or paint. And he couldn't carry the inventory in his small building that the big boys did, either. If Ben wanted to survive in business, it was time to start from scratch.

But he couldn't do that. Both his grandfather and his father had managed the hardware store in Friedens. Could he really call his dad in Arizona and tell him he was running the family business into the ground? He couldn't even face telling Claire that, much less his father.

Maybe if he'd gotten a pro football contract he could have changed his father's assumption that he'd take over the hardware store. But by marrying Claire and starting a family so young, he'd done in his college career as a ball player. And at that point he wasn't such a standout that he could have gone pro. Without that option, he'd gone home and drifted into managing the hardware store the way his father had expected. Selling out now felt more like chickening out.

Then there was that stupid bet he'd gotten himself roped into. How on earth was he going to even try to run the house for thirty minutes, much less thirty days? He wasn't even real sure where they kept the bread. He sort of knew how to run the washing machine, if they still had the same one they had when Kyle was born. That was probably the last time he'd washed clothes.

No, he had to face the fact that he was much better at handling a balance sheet than a bed sheet. He knew much more about the kind of washer that went into a faucet than the kind that did the laundry. What knowledge he did have of household appliances was how to fix them if they broke, not how to use them when they worked. And he'd taken a dare to run the house for a month just to prove to Claire that he knew what he was doing.

Who was he fooling? It was time to turn off the TV and get rid of the sports section. Time to go into the kitchen and apologize to Claire for what he'd said to her. Then he could tell her about the business problems he was having, had been having for months but was just now coming to terms with. She would understand because he could tell her anything. Hadn't he always told her everything?

No, not always. He kept a lot to himself these days so as not to worry her. There were the mistakes he made, the things he couldn't change. And there was his need to protect her from the world—a world he knew she wasn't up to handling.

Besides, if he went in there and told Claire everything, the first thing she would want to do was seek guidance from the Lord. It was a natural thing for her—maybe the thing he envied more than anything else about her, even her ease with the boys and the house. And it was the one thing Ben wasn't about to do anymore. He'd managed to hide his loss of trust from Claire, just as he'd managed to keep his business failures to himself.

He could almost imagine being able to handle Claire's knowing about him selling the hardware store. Admitting the depth of his failure wouldn't be pretty, but he could do it if he had to. But he could not imagine the look on her face if he told her he didn't pray anymore unless he was saying grace at the table.

His Bible was almost musty from lack of use, and his memory of Scripture was just as bad. But as bad as the emptiness he felt was the thought of admitting it to anybody. Didn't it say there was something wrong with him? That he'd lost something so precious? And he didn't even know how or when he'd lost it. It was as if his faith had trickled away when he wasn't looking. Then when he went to look for it, nothing was there.

That wasn't even the worst admission he would have to make. Most of all, he couldn't imagine what Claire would say if he told her what he felt; that this distance between him and God was just fine with him. She would never forgive him for that. Some things were forgivable in Claire's eyes, he knew. Probably even the thought that he might be fooling around on the side. Though damaging, she could live with it. But to know that her husband was the ultimate fraud in the faith department? No, it was better to sit here reading the same box scores, listening to the game drone on.

Chapter Five

~~

Claire was ready to go to bed. It wasn't all that late, but she was tired. It was probably the aggravation of the day rather than actual exhaustion that made her want the familiar comfort of her room. Now her only debate was whether to roust Ben from his recliner to bring him upstairs, as well.

Even when they weren't getting along as well as usual, he was part of that familiar comfort. Thinking that made her pause. Is that what they meant to each other these days? Familiar comfort? Heavens, she hoped not. Surely there was something more, something like the fire that seemed to spark all the time when they were younger.

Marriage changed as people got older. She knew that. But she wasn't ready to settle for familiar and comfortable yet in her marriage, even after sixteen years. And if his actions this week were any indicator, Ben wasn't settling for being familiar, either. She couldn't imagine that there was anything really going on between him and Marcy from high school, except a business deal of some sort.

But when had things changed enough that even the business deals didn't get discussed with her? Claire walked up the stairs alone, trying to sort out that puzzle in her head. When was the last time Ben had brought a work-related problem to her?

Maybe never, she had to admit. Ben considered the hardware store his baby. Whether he thought he was being kind protecting her from the problems he faced there, or just sure that she wouldn't have any insight, he kept those problems to himself. If he really got stuck somehow, he called his dad in Arizona, but Claire could count the times he'd done that on the fingers of one hand.

Claire paused on the landing, surprised by a realization. Maybe this was why she felt so led to The Caring Closet. She wanted more out of life; to diversify their partnership, as she'd told Ben before. Perhaps if she had some experience running a business, even in a volunteer way, Ben would see her as someone to discuss business with. She was ready and eager to learn.

Thank you, Father, she prayed silently. What a

wonderful chance to do something for the Lord and learn lessons for herself at the same time. She hurried to her room, anxious now to find the books she'd checked out of the library on small business management. She had studying to do, and suddenly it sounded like fun. Going up to her room could wait. She wasn't tired anymore.

She took her books down to the living room and settled in on one corner of the couch. Even though it was warm enough to have the windows closed, she could hear the boys outside on the driveway playing roller hockey with friends.

In the room, a Cardinal baseball game was on the television, while Ben dozed in the recliner with his remote control still in his lap. Tucking her legs up on the sofa, Claire looked over at her husband. Asleep, he looked younger. Those lines around his eyes vanished.

It would be nice to be able to rub away those lines and the near-permanent crease in his forehead by taking on some of the burdens he bore. But it would take a lot of talking on her part, and proof that she really knew what she was talking about, before Ben was ready to share any of those burdens. Better to get down to business and start learning.

Claire felt like whistling or humming while she

read. This was the start of something new and different and wonderful. She could feel it.

Ben startled himself awake. Was it the end of the ball game that woke him up, or the back door slamming to let in a herd of rowdy boys? Whichever it was, neither seemed to bother Claire. She stayed at the end of the couch, absorbed in her library book.

That must mean it was one of those love stories she always checked out. Ben smiled, watching her absently twirl a lock of honey-flecked brown hair while she read. Still his dreamer, his romantic. Maybe he didn't have to worry so much about her and her new ideas, after all.

"Hey, Mom," Trent called from the kitchen. "Are there more ice pops someplace? We're hot and there's six of us."

Claire looked up from her reading, letting loose her hair. "What? More pops? No, just those in the freezer in the kitchen. I think there's a box of fudge bars in there someplace, though. If you finish all the ice pops, you can each have one of those. But eat them outside, okay? And then make sure everybody goes home. I don't want any moms calling me to see where their boys are—it's getting late."

"Sure." There was more rattling and clattering in the kitchen.

Claire stood. "And Trent—?" The door slammed shut, and she winced. "I guess I don't really need to tell him to share equally with his brother and his friends, do I? Surely they've outgrown squabbling with each other."

Ben shrugged. "Do they ever outgrow that? That's the drawback of being an only child, as far as I'm concerned. I don't know what's normal with those two because I never had anybody to fight with."

"Or to share with, either," Claire said, coming over to where he still sat in the recliner, and running a hand through his hair. Her soft caress gave him the urge to purr like a cat. "Maybe that's why you're so closemouthed about work."

The urge to purr died in his throat. Did she have to bring that up again? He rolled his neck to get out the cricks that sleeping in the recliner had brought on, gently dislodging her fingers from his hair. "Maybe. Or maybe I enjoy keeping some things to myself. Do we really have to go through this again?"

The sparkle left her eyes. "No, I guess we don't. But I want to be more than the ice-pop monitor around here, Ben. I want you to feel like you can actually come home and share with me."

He'd argue that he shared with her plenty, except it wasn't true. Not in the way Claire wanted him to. What was she waving in front of him? He looked at the book in her hand, surprise growing as he read the title. Her library book wasn't one of those flowery love stories, after all. It was some big thick thing about small business management. Nuts, maybe she was more serious about this whole closet mission thing than he realized.

"You know that getting a bunch of women to hold a rummage sale at church is a bunch different than running a business," he began as gently as possible.

A frown creased her forehead. "I've told you more than once, this isn't like a rummage sale. It's going to be a long, ongoing project. Something serious that I can help people with, and learn from. Something I'm excited about doing."

Great, just what he needed; to set her off again. "I can see that." Ben eased himself out of the chair. They weren't going to be on the same frequency for this discussion no matter how many times they had it. "I don't want you to get in over your head and be overwhelmed. That's all I'm trying to say."

That was apparently the wrong thing to say. Claire looked more peeved than before. "Who says I'm going to get in over my head? And no matter what, I won't be any more overwhelmed

than you will be the first time you try making out
a grocery list.''

His stomach lurched as if he'd started down the
longest hill on a steep roller coaster. ''Grocery list?
Aw, Claire, you're not really going to hold me to
that bet, are you?''

Now she was smiling. ''I sure am. I'm serious
about that double-dog dare. And I hope you are,
too.'' The smile got even wider. ''In fact, if you
want to make things more interesting, I know how
to do it.''

He came toward her, reaching for her waist. ''So
do I, but I have a feeling we're not agreeing.''

She sidestepped him neatly, but at least she was
still smiling. ''You've got that right. Watch where
you put those hands, mister. No, I have a second
suggestion for you.''

Hmm. He might still be able to derail the serious
nature of this discussion. And that could only benefit him in the long run. ''I didn't know you'd
given me a first one.''

Her hands on his shoulders were welcome, even
if she was still holding that darn book in one hand.
It was heavy and poked him right about collarbone
level.

''Benjamin, you know what I mean. At least,
you would if you let me get a whole sentence in.''

Her expression got a little more serious. This distraction thing wasn't working.

Claire put down the book on an end table, and came back to face him, hands on his shoulders again. "I know you don't want to tell me what's going on with Marcy. And I understand you think you've got my best interest at heart, even though I think you're wrong. *And* I still want to prove to you that I could be more help than you believe. So I'll make you a deal. You try your hand at my usual household chores, and I won't ask about your business dealings for the next month."

"Not once?" This sounded too good to be true. All he had to do was putter around the house, and she'd leave him alone. This could be a sweet deal. How hard could it be, really?

She shook her head, sending her hair bouncing in a way that made it difficult for Ben to concentrate on what she was saying. "Not once. However, if you admit defeat at the end of the month with the house or any time before that, I get to come in to the hardware store and get the inside scoop on everything."

She still knew his soft spots. "You drive a hard bargain," he growled. That was going to get him in trouble, but he couldn't help it. "I'll even go you one better. If you last a month letting me run the house my way while you do this thing at church, I'll take you into the store and—''

''Tell me everything I've ever wanted to know?'' Claire broke in. ''Tell me what you and Marcy are cooking up? Fill me in on your business from square one?''

That wasn't what he had in mind, but it was a possibility. He couldn't imagine having to hold up his end of the bargain, anyway. Claire would cave long before he did.

Better to throw her off guard by actually agreeing with her. ''You've got it. Although I was going to offer to take you away for a weekend. After the month you're going to put us through, we'll both need the rest.''

''Maybe *you* will, mister.'' The sparkle was back in her eyes, making Ben yearn to pull her more securely into his arms, whether or not the boys could see in the windows from the driveway. Better to know their parents still cared about each other. But Claire was too quick for him. She was already out of his grasp and halfway up the stairs before he could cross the room.

''Yes, you may need the rest, but I'm looking forward to the challenge. I think I may do my own laundry, though. I like my clothes to stay the same size I bought them. And the same color.''

A month of this? Ben wasn't sure he could manage a week. He wondered how long that box of ice pops was going to last outside. Not long enough for him to talk with Claire. The guys would be in the house wrestling over evening showers long before he had a chance.

Maybe it was for the best. If he was really going to win this bet, he needed all his strength and a clear head to figure out how to handle things around the house. Asking where they kept the vacuum cleaner and other important things, like the number for the pizza place, probably wasn't a good way to start out. He followed his wife up the stairs, hoping the fudge bars held out for a few minutes, anyway.

Claire took one last look at her notes. Now that she was sitting in the big meeting room at church, the yellow pad in front of her on the table didn't look as full as it had at home. Where was everybody? When she'd called all the women who said they were interested in working on The Caring Closet, she'd gotten a lot of positive responses.

Now that they actually had a time and place to meet and get started on this, it was a different story. Claire was alone in the large room. Of course, she was a few minutes early. Maybe everybody else was just running on a summer time schedule.

When she heard footsteps down the hall, and people actually coming in the door, Claire felt enormous relief. But her cheerful greeting almost died on her lips when she turned around and saw who was joining her.

"That *is* decaffeinated coffee in the pot, isn't it?" Peggy Grady asked.

"And nobody's put out hot water for tea," her sister Patsy Grady Trump said. It came out a little like a whine, but then, anything Patsy said seemed to. It was the one way to tell the twins apart. Peggy had spent most of her sixty-eight years on the planet investigating possible problems, and her sister just went straight to complaining about them.

And naturally, as retired schoolteachers, they had all the time in the world to come help run this project. Claire found herself leaping up and heading toward the sink. Her well-honed sense of guilt couldn't keep her sitting. "I guess I forgot about the hot water," she said, going to fill the second coffeepot. "And I'm pretty sure that is decaf. It came out of the green can in the kitchen, anyway."

Peggy sniffed in displeasure. "I suppose that's as sure as we can get. Maybe I'll be brave and have a cup." She looked at the pot, then sat down at the conference table, eyeing it suspiciously. "Although last time I took somebody else's word for it, I was up all night."

"Watching those rude late-night television shows." Her sister's displeasure at having her own routine disturbed was plain. The two had lived together in the old family home since Patsy's husband had died ten years earlier.

While she filled the pot with water at the sink, and poured it through the small coffeemaker to make a pot of hot water, Claire prayed to herself. She asked for strength to do the task at hand, and patience, which she normally didn't have enough of anyway, to deal with squabbling siblings. Wasn't it bad enough that she had to deal with that at home all the time? Now her perfect project at church was going to be challenged by the Grump Sisters.

She scolded herself for using Ben's private name for the two women who were the backbone of the church. Surely they'd have more help in a minute. And this wasn't her project, anyway. It belonged to the Lord. Her job was to use the people He called to action.

That pile of notes still didn't look very substantial when she got back to it. "Was there anybody else in the parking lot when you got here?" she asked the sisters, hoping for more companionship soon.

Patsy nodded, which didn't disturb her tightly permed waves of silver hair. "I think a small fleet of those minivans were pulling up. And all late as usual. Don't get started yet unless you want to go over everything twice. You know they'll all have to stop for a cold soda out of the machine in the youth room."

"And there's never enough diet, or enough quarters between them," Peggy chimed in.

This might be a very long morning. No, Claire corrected herself, it would *definitely* be a long morning. Now she had to find the ways to make it not only long but also workable. She had a job to do and it was time to start doing it, with or without the help of the Grump Sisters.

"Claire?" Mrs. Perkins, the harried church secretary, sounded even more harried than usual over the telephone system intercom. "Are you in there?"

Claire walked to the doorway where the phone lights were blinking and punched the reply button on the complicated phone system. "Right here. Call for me?"

"Sure is. Sorry to bother you, but it's Trent. And he said something about stuff coming out of the dishwasher."

Wonderful. What kind of stuff would that be? "Thanks." Claire punched in the button to connect to the house. "Trent? What's going on?"

"Dad got us all doing chores, and one of mine

was dishes. And, well, is there supposed to be foam coming out of the dishwasher? Because I don't remember that part.''

He sounded worried. Claire had to grin a little at the mental image of her tall son watching the rabid dishwasher. As if on cue, four women all came through the doorway of the room, all talking at once and milling for places at the table.

"Find a seat, and I'll be there in a minute," Claire called, one hand over the phone. "I'm back," she told Trent. "And no, there's not supposed to be foam coming out of the dishwasher. But it's really not my problem, guy, it's Dad's. Call and ask him how much soap he put in there. And what kind."

There was silence on the other end of the phone for a minute. And then a laugh. "Oh, man. Do you think he didn't know the difference between the stuff we use in the sink and the stuff for the dishwasher? Hey, at least there'll be enough foam to wash the whole kitchen floor. Kyle ought to thank him, because that was his job."

Claire had to share Trent's laughter. "I hope he sees it that way. And remember, unless something's on fire or it involves blood, call Dad instead today. He's the house person in charge for the next thirty days. Got it?"

"Got it," Trent said, then hung up. Claire turned

back to the table, where six women were still talking at once. It was time to get down to real business.

"Who wants to give the opening prayer?" Claire asked brightly, going to her seat at the end of the table. Compared to a kitchen full of soapsuds and whatever other crises were at home, this was going to be a breeze.

Chapter Six

So far this had been possibly the worst day of Ben's life. And it wasn't even three in the afternoon yet. No wonder Claire always said she liked winter better than summer. How did she get anything done in the summertime at all if she had to handle this many miniature disasters, referee fights and answer absurd questions all day?

At least she knew it all face to face and in person. It was bad enough knowing that everybody had to be someplace that they couldn't walk to sometime this afternoon and that they were out of milk. Knowing it via the seventh phone call of the day was less than pleasant.

So at least he could answer that nagging question he had about what Claire did all day. And given all the negotiating, refereeing and planning she had to do every day just to get through, maybe she had more business management skills than he had given her credit for.

When the phone rang at his elbow again, just as he'd gotten the power tools inventory list worked out, he didn't bother to answer it. Let Pete pick it up. Or let nobody pick it up. He just didn't care.

The phone stopped ringing, but before he could be happy about that, Pete appeared in the doorway. "Marcy McKinnon on the line. She says you're hard to get hold of."

"I'll bet she does today. Thanks, Pete." He picked up the phone, trying to mentally adjust his game face while he did so. Naturally, the one time he hadn't answered it was something important. "Marcy? What can I do for you?"

Her answering chuckle was smooth and throaty. "So you are alive, after all. And at your desk. I thought you might have taken the day off to go fishing or something. Haven't you ever heard of call waiting?"

Ben could hear both amusement and aggravation in her voice. "That's just for you high-powered corporate types, isn't it? What would a simple hardware store owner like me need with call waiting?"

"If it takes ten calls to get in touch with you

just to move a business deal along, you could use it. I hope you've given some thought to what we talked about.''

All too much. But he wasn't about to tell Marcy that right off the bat. "I still have some checking to do. This is a big deal. I mean, this is my family business we're talking about. My grandpa and my dad both poured their lives into this building. I'm not about to turn it over to strangers on a whim.''

"Of course not," Marcy murmured. "Give it all the time you like, within reason. I'm sure you have more questions I could answer. What about coming to the big city and letting me take you to lunch and discuss things?''

"That sounds pretty good. What day did you have in mind?''

"There's a businessman's special at the ballpark on Friday. Why don't you come up then? We can see the game, use the company box and have a little entertainment while we discuss things.''

Marcy had done her homework. She'd found the quickest way to entice him into coming into the city. A baseball game and a ballpark hot dog won every time over some stuffy lunch in a fancy restaurant. "I guess so. Where would you want to meet?''

"Come by the office about ten. That will give

us time to talk before we have to leave for the game. Do you know how to get here?''

"Sure." He could figure it out, anyway. "See you then." It was only after Ben hung up and reached for the desk calendar to note the appointment that he realized he hadn't given a thought to his home responsibilities. He had no idea whether there was anything going on Friday that he needed to be a part of.

Grabbing a pencil, he shrugged. Nothing could be that important or timely, could it? He'd just check with the guys tonight when he got home. Besides, if he really got stuck, Claire would bail him out. She'd only really done much on The Caring Closet thing for the last two days. How deeply involved could she have gotten in that amount of time?

All his answers came at dinner, and none of them was what Ben wanted to hear. Of course, the general atmosphere in the kitchen didn't promote a lot of peace and harmony, anyway.

"This is dinner?" Kyle asked, looking at the scene. Ben tried to see it through his son's eyes for a moment.

Okay, so there weren't any real dishes. But carryout pizza tasted the same in foam bowls with Christmas designs as it would on real plates. "You have a problem with it?'' Ben didn't mean to growl, but it had been a rotten day so far.

"I guess not. What's to drink?''

"There's tea and plenty of ice.'' Judging from Kyle's suspicious expression, it wasn't quite right.

"Where's my cup?''

"In the dishwasher. Rinsing off again.'' For the third time. How could one soap mistake make so many slimy dishes? "Does it matter that much?''

Kyle shrugged and sat down, as Trent and Claire came into the kitchen. Trent stood looking at the table, his brow furrowing the way his brother's had. "Okay.'' He sounded dubious. But he didn't say anything more and he sat down.

"Could you pass the, uh, paper towels?'' Claire asked Kyle. Guess that was her way of pointing out they had no paper napkins. Cute. How was he supposed to know they were out of paper napkins? There were dozens of little tricks, and Ben felt clueless about all of them right now.

Ben said grace, confident that at least he got that right. He let everybody dig in to the pizza and eat for a few minutes in silence before he started making conversation.

"So, I hope nobody has big plans for Friday. I made an appointment in St. Louis and I can't play chauffeur.''

Trent stopped with pizza halfway to his mouth. "Friday, Dad?"

Well, that was a great beginning. "What's wrong with Friday?"

Trent spoke very slowly and clearly, as if he were sure his father was deaf. "If I don't get my sports physical done, I can't start two-a-days with the junior varsity football squad in two weeks."

That was all? "So we'll just reschedule. How hard can that be?"

Claire snorted indelicately. "You have no idea how far ahead I had to call just to get this appointment, do you? And Kyle goes in then, too, for his allergy shot. That's every other Friday morning."

As if you didn't know was her unspoken finish to that sentence, and it made Ben feel more foolish than before. He *didn't* know. There was a whole layer of stuff in his family's life that he didn't know. It wouldn't make him look any better to ask how long Kyle had been taking allergy shots. Or why the doctor was so hard to get in to see that you apparently had to have an engraved invitation.

"You couldn't just—" he started, but saw Claire emphatically shake her head.

"No, I couldn't. Not unless you want to admit defeat right now instead of waiting the rest of the month. I'm supposed to meet Nessa Friday morning. And the meeting is at a church ten miles from here in Union, to show me what a program that's been up and running a while looks like. Ben, she went to a lot of trouble to set this up. You could have checked first.''

Yeah, he probably could have. Just like he could stop by the gas station to get directions next time he was lost. But it just wasn't part of his character to do either one. "Give me the timing on all this again.''

Trent looked a little relieved and started eating pizza.

"Sports physical at nine, allergy shots at ten. If you're in with Trent for the physical, they might sneak Kyle in early so you can do both at once.''

At least Claire didn't have any problems sharing her information. And she knew all the tricks.

This might work yet. All he had to do was call Marcy back and tell her he'd just meet her at the stadium. It would be more of a hassle, but he'd still look good in everybody's eyes. "Okay. I think I can handle that.''

"Better than you handled doing dishes, I hope,'' he heard Trent mutter. If his son hadn't been right on the mark, Ben would have lost his temper.

Still, he needed to stay in control here. Leader of the pack and all that.

"I heard that.'' He tried to sound calm, not barking. "Just for that, you can help out. When you're done with dinner, go look in the pantry and the refrigerator and make a list of what we're missing. Then Kyle and I will go grocery shopping." He added that last bit to quiet his snickering younger son, who had been enjoying his brother's discomfort at being caught mouthing off.

"Don't forget to add paper napkins to the list," Claire said, pointing to the roll of paper towels on the table.

How could she just sit there and smile all through this. Ben was glad he could provide this much entertainment his first day on the job.

Claire held her breath as she listened to the phone. After three rings she was ready to hang up, but someone answered.

"Hello—"

Gloria had caller ID, so she at least knew what household was calling.

"Claire? If you wanted to talk to your dad, you're out of luck tonight—"

"No, I want you this time."

"What's up?" Gloria sounded surprised.

"I need reinforcements." Claire looked down at the list in her hand. "This Caring Closet project is getting out of hand. Don't tell my husband I said that, because he's sure I'll be a miserable failure."

"I can't see that happening. But what's the mat-

ter with the volunteers that signed up for the project? When I looked at the sign-up sheet at church,
it seemed pretty full.''

''I had five people show up today besides me.
Peggy and Patsy came first.''

She could hear a faint chuckle from Gloria's end
of the line. ''I can see some of the problem already.
They do add a special dimension to any project
there. And the rest?''

Claire told her. She was already ready to admit
that between the Grump sisters and the minivan
squad, she might never unify everybody into a
team.

That was the hardest part of competing with
Ben. She didn't have anybody to bounce ideas off.
In any normal situation, she'd wait until bedtime
and ask Ben all these questions. But when he was
part of the problem, she missed his wide shoulders
to carry part of her burden.

''Hey, with your dad gone tonight, I've got time
to talk this over. Want to come out for some lemonade and girl talk?''

Claire felt her spirits rise. ''And how. Let me
grab my car keys and write a note for the guys,
and I'll see you soon.''

Gloria's kitchen was wonderful, Claire thought
as she entered half an hour later. Maybe this was
what Claire's would look like someday when there

weren't boys trooping through it all the time: crisp white curtains, lovely little touches here and there that were feminine but not overpowering, and a real cookie jar full of cookies. If Claire had a cookie jar, there would only be crumbs.

Claire sat at the round maple table, surrounded by glowing copper and brass that all shone to a high finish. There weren't even any fingerprints on the refrigerator door.

"I know what you're thinking, but it doesn't always look this good," Gloria said, putting two icy glasses of lemonade on the table. "If nothing else, there are usually Tyler's and Mikayla's handprints on everything three feet tall and under. Lori says I spoil them, and I suppose she's right. They get to do things at Grandma's house that they wouldn't at home. But they keep me well supplied with refrigerator art."

"I miss that part," Claire admitted. "The guys are too big to bring home artwork from school most of the time. My refrigerator is mostly a place for magnets that hold sports schedules and the like."

"We've got a few of those, too. There's Tyler's T-ball schedule, and Mike and Lori are on a coed softball team. So that doesn't necessarily end— But you didn't come to admire my refrigerator.

What's on your mind?'' Gloria settled comfortably in her chair.

Where did she start? ''Everything. And it's going to be hard to make sense of it all at once. I don't know where to begin. How well do you know the Grady sisters?''

''Well enough to give you sympathy if you're working with them on a long-term project. Hank already told me about this Caring Closet. Which I think is a wonderful idea, by the way. And I'm tickled to death that they didn't come ask me right away to head the project or something, now that I'm joining the church.''

Claire's heart sank, leaving a trail as cool as the lemonade she was sipping. It pooled in an icy puddle at the pit of her stomach. This was sure starting off well. ''So you're not interested in The Caring Closet?''

Gloria held up one hand. She pointed upward with her index finger, sending glints from the new gold-and-diamond wedding set on her ring finger dancing into the shadowy corners of the kitchen. ''Not interested in running the thing. I didn't say I wouldn't be interested in helping out. And I can give you a few tips on ways around Peggy and Patsy. Or, at least, hints to keep them busy enough that they're not at each other's throats more than once or twice a week.''

Claire smiled. "Great. For a minute I thought I came out here on a fool's errand. Which I may have, but at least there's cold lemonade. And real paper napkins." Gloria's raised eyebrow begged her to explain that last statement, and she did. By the time she'd told her everything, both women had their shoes kicked off and had worked through several of those paper napkins. They were good for mopping up after laughter-induced lemonade spills and tears, as well. Claire felt as if she could really have a true ally in Gloria.

It was nearly ten o'clock when Claire looked at the time again. "Oh. I have got to get home to the boys."

Gloria smiled. "Do you think you'll have paper napkins?"

Claire shook her head. "Not a chance." She stood up and hugged Gloria. "Thanks for listening. And talking. And just being here. I promise, I won't ask you to do too much on The Caring Closet."

"It sounds like my kind of project. Let me know how I can help the best."

Claire stepped back. "You can probably help most by offering me cookies and lemonade once in a while, and a sympathetic ear. Of course, some of those dynamite suits you wear that you're tired of wouldn't hurt, either."

Gloria laughed. "Now, there's an argument for a new wardrobe if I ever heard one. Won't your father be thrilled?"

"Just don't tell him it was my idea," Claire said, heading for the door. Just what she needed— to be the cause of a marital spat about money. But she doubted that would happen any time soon. Both Hank and Gloria had come into this marriage as independent adults. Hank probably would never know how much Gloria spent on clothing in a month. And if she was lucky, Gloria would never know what he spent on fishing tackle.

Claire mused about what part money played in this whole bid for independence as she drove home from Gloria's house. Did she envy her stepmother because she was an independent woman of means? Yes, a little, if she was honest with herself.

It would be good to spend money once in a while without feeling as if she had to account for it to Ben. Not that he ever complained. But he was the only source of money for the household, other than a tiny savings account in Claire's name, set aside from an inheritance from her mother. Ben hardly ever let her touch that. That was always the emergency fund, and for Ben, no emergency was so big that he couldn't handle it himself.

Claire had to admit that having a little money of her own would be good. Being the chief cook, bottle washer and chauffeur for everybody around the place was rewarding, but not in a financial way. And there had to be half a dozen ways she could make money using the skills she'd picked up over the years in her volunteer work.

Maybe The Caring Closet was a way to prove to Ben that she was more independent than he thought. That she could do something besides washing clothes or baking cookies. And she really did feel led to do this after she'd prayed about it. This wasn't just a selfish whim on her part to do something that would make herself look good. This was a way to grow both in her skills and in the Lord.

Ben's truck was in the garage when she got home, but there was nobody out in the driveway playing roller hockey or shooting hoops. That was odd on a nice night, even this late.

She could hear laughter coming from the kitchen. The sound made her smile. Maybe the three of them had learned something together this evening. They had worked as a team and done something new, going to the grocery store and coming back with food for the week. And now, putting it all away, they seemed to be having a good time together. Perhaps this was going to work out better than she thought.

She stepped inside the kitchen and changed her

mind instantly. Chaos ruled. The guys had bought groceries. At least, they'd bought something, judging from the number of sacks on the kitchen table. What she could see poking out of them was mostly cookies and chips and two-liter bottles of soda. No paper napkins in sight. Fortunately, there was nothing perishable left out, either, like ice cream or milk, so perhaps they had a little more common sense than she gave them credit for.

There was a huge bag leaning against one kitchen chair. What did they need that came in a sack that size? Claire looked at the label. Premium Puppy Kibble. *Puppy kibble?* Oh, no. This was *not* happening.

In answer, a large furry bundle of energy raced around the table yapping, and flung itself at Claire, knocking her over in its delight. She sat on the floor and had her face washed with a large wet tongue, huge paws planted on her chest. Was this a puppy or a Shetland pony?

"Hey, Mom," Kyle said, coming around the table himself, grinning like a jack-o'-lantern. "Look what we got at the grocery store. He was free, and Dad says we can keep him. Isn't that too cool for words?"

Chapter Seven

"This is a puppy?" Claire managed to get out in a voice that sounded strangled even to her. "It's awfully big for a puppy, isn't it?" She eased the creature off her chest and tried to dry her ear, where she was sure she was now missing an earring. Would gold give a beast that size a tummy ache?

"The guy outside the grocery store said he's only four months old. He's not full grown at all yet," Kyle said, grabbing the beast's collar. "Are ya, Tiger? Huh? Are ya, boy?"

Tiger's giant tail thumped inches from Claire's face as the dog danced with Kyle. "Why was he for sale in front of the grocery store? And what possessed you to get him?"

"He wasn't for sale," Kyle crowed, letting the beast wash his face with abandon. "He was free. And Dad said we could bring him home as long as he was in charge."

Ben's smile dared her to say anything different. His blue eyes flashed signals at her; that pearly grin dared her to speak. Claire's fingers itched to strangle her handsome husband. She was really stuck. If she told them to take this monster back immediately to where they'd found him, she would avert disaster. But Ben would consider himself the winner by default in their contest. She knew how his mind worked: her issuing a direct order like that over his head would signal that she was taking back the reins.

So which was worse? Having a puppy the size of a small car or calling it quits this early in the game? If she sent the puppy back she might never get to find out exactly what Marcy was doing at the hardware store. And Ben would feel no need to share the other things about the store with her, either.

On the other hand, having this monster frolic through her house with paws the size of dinner plates and a tail like a bullwhip was a disaster waiting to happen. How would she get The Caring Closet going with this beast in the middle of everything?

She watched Kyle and Trent for a moment, their faces alight with happiness as they enjoyed the antics of this big, awkward pup. This was the reason she'd never let them bring home a dog. All of them got attached to things so quickly, much more than she did. She didn't want a big smelly, noisy beast in the house. A grown man and two growing boys made enough mess around the place, and plenty of noise. But seeing them with the soft, goofy animal, even for ten minutes, told her she couldn't possibly send the pet back.

He filled some place in their hearts, even though he didn't do anything for her personally. And Ben looked so delighted with his choice. It would be fun to see his expression in a moment when she said they could keep this four-legged monster.

She got up off the floor and brushed at her clothing. She was probably covered in dog hair already. "Okay, but this means that you guys and Dad are really in charge of this dog." Ben's jaw went a little slack with surprise. For a moment she wanted to waltz over and kiss him, just to surprise him more. But she stood her ground, watching him flounder.

"He'll need to be walked and taken outside a lot and cleaned up after. He'll need baths and brushing and feeding. And he's a baby still, even if he is huge. He'll cry at night for his mom and his littermates. Somebody will have to get up with him. And it will not be me. Do you three think you can really handle that?''

"Sure," chorused Trent and Kyle. They looked at their dad for his assurance that he was part of this deal. Claire could see the wheels turning in Ben's brain. What could he do now? Ben had obviously expected that bringing home this monster would push her over the edge. That she'd dispatch the dog before any of them went to bed, and life would be back to normal. Now he was responsible for over fifty pounds of puppy.

It was almost worth the work Claire knew was ahead of her.

His answering grin was weak. It tickled her to see it. Almost made her feel sorry for him, but not sorry enough to say anything.

"Sure, I guess." He didn't sound terribly sure of himself. The look he flashed her said she was right on target with her assessment of the situation.

"I don't suppose anybody thought to get a crate big enough for this guy," Claire said. Tiger seemed to know they were talking about him. He bounded between Kyle and Claire, kissing one hand and then the other in puppy joy.

"Crate? What does he need that for? He can sleep with us, can't he?" Trent rumpled the sleek fur on the pup's head.

"He most certainly cannot." Claire had to stand her ground with this one. "Especially not as a four-month-old puppy. Puppies that young aren't fully house-trained yet, no matter what their size. I don't want this huge beast having midnight accidents in your bedrooms. If he doesn't have a crate, he needs blankets in the kitchen or the laundry room."

Kyle wrinkled his brow in thought. Like his father, he was pretty inventive. If anybody could come up with a creative solution tonight, it would probably be Kyle. In a moment the wrinkles cleared, and he smiled. "I know. Do we still have those old baby gate things downstairs, Mom?"

"Probably. But the kitchen doorway is too wide for them." She hated to burst his bubble so quickly.

"No problem. That wasn't my idea, anyway. I was thinking about the pantry. If we moved things like the pots and pans down to the low shelves, and the boxes and things he might be able to open up where he couldn't, we could gate him in there. It would be like his own fort. He'd love it."

He probably would, Claire thought with chagrin. Especially nibbling on things in the pantry that the boys didn't expect he could reach. It sounded like an awful idea to her. But before she could argue, Ben started talking.

"You're going to have to do a lot of work to

make this happen. And we still have to put away all the groceries. But those two jobs could be combined so we only have to move things once. Trent, you and Kyle go into the pantry and start rearranging. I'll take everything we bought out of the bags and put it on the kitchen table. Then when you're ready, we can put the gate up, put Tiger in his new fort and pass in the stuff that needs to be put away.''

A man with a plan. Claire watched the mayhem in front of her for a minute, with the three guys bumping into each other and the pup weaving around all of them, and she laughed. "Have a great time, guys. I'm going to go take a bubble bath and read my management books. Don't use any of the good blankets in the linen closet for this hound. Only the ones in the stack in the basement."

"Fine," Ben said. He sounded distracted as he tried to unload groceries without the dog eating them. It was almost entertaining enough to stay down here and watch. But the bubble bath called, and Gloria's admonishments still rang in her ears. The older woman had urged her to use this whole situation for growth for them all. And if this wasn't a growth moment, she didn't know what was.

This wasn't how he had expected to spend the night. Ben lay stock-still, staring up at the ceiling of the bedroom. So he wasn't hearing the stupid peeper frogs for a change. No, they were totally drowned out by the howling and whining of that huge puppy downstairs in the pantry. What had ever possessed him to let the guys take that thing home? If Claire knew that the puppy, boys and groceries had all ridden home in the truck bed instead of in the cab, she would have his hide. As it was, she hadn't said a word to him since she'd gone upstairs, letting him handle getting that mutt to bed for the night.

Feeling her still form next to him was driving him crazy. This was usually the best part of his day. They talked over problems and successes. He could touch her without the guys watching every move. The years fell away, and the girl he married often slid into his arms.

But now she was over on her side of the bed, nearly to the edge, silent. And he was listening to that dog. In about two minutes he was going to get out of this bed and throw that animal outside where he couldn't hear the whining and moaning.

Suddenly it was quiet. The puppy gave one short whine, then stopped. Ben couldn't even hear peeper frogs, thanks to Claire's insistence that the air-conditioning needed to stay on for the mutt. She wasn't concerned about the big moose being too hot in the night, but had argued something about "white noise" being good for him, whatever that meant.

Had the silly animal finally reached up high enough on a pantry shelf to reach something edible? Or maybe he'd just finally swallowed something that wasn't really edible but was within reach, anyway, and choked. Ben slipped out of bed, sure that the silence meant disaster. With his luck so far this week, how could it mean anything else?

There was a soft light in the kitchen cast by the small bulb over the stove. In its faint light Ben could see a large shape on the pantry floor. Surely it was too large a shape to be only that dog. What had the kids named him? *Tiger.* He was kind of tiger-striped with his brindle coat, the mixed black and tan that seemed to hint of boxer and Great Dane heritage.

As he peered into the pantry, set off by its baby gate, the shape raised a head. "Dad?" somebody called softly from the pile. It was Kyle.

It took a moment to get over being startled by somebody talking from the dog pile. "You sleeping with the puppy?"

"Just for a little while. He sounded so lonely. I remember when I used to go take a sleeping bag and sleep on Trent's floor when I felt like I wanted company. That was before I knew about Jesus always being awake to watch out for me. And I figure there's just about no way to tell a puppy about Jesus, so I'll just sleep with him for a while until he grows up some and gets less lonely."

The simplicity of his eleven-year-old's explanation nearly ripped Ben's heart out. It was all he could do not to ask Kyle to tell him again about Jesus. To remind him of all the promises God made to always be with us, until all he could do was believe them like a child. Like his child, lying on the pantry floor with his new puppy.

He couldn't say any of that. Leaning against the kitchen doorframe, Ben swallowed the lump in his throat. It had been so very, very long since things were that simple for him. He actually envied the boy with his arm around the puppy. And it did quiet down the dog. Tiger was curled up next to Kyle, breathing softly and slowly.

"I guess if that's what works, it's a pretty good idea. If he wakes up and cries, take him outside, okay, son?"

"Sure. I'll bet he learns everything like that real fast. He's awful smart." The pride in his voice made Ben glad that he hadn't goaded Claire into taking the puppy back to the grocery store parking lot. He remembered having dogs as a boy, and all the responsibility they had taught him. He didn't want these guys to grow up without the same experience.

"He looks like a smart dog." Ben turned and went back up the stairs. In the kitchen he could hear Kyle settling back in with the puppy.

"Everything okay down there?" Claire asked softly, as he slid into bed.

It was so good to hear her sleepy voice. Ben relaxed, knowing he could talk to her. "For now. Kyle's sleeping with the dog. And before you say anything about that, I don't like the idea, either, but the dog loves it. And it may be the only way any of us gets any sleep tonight."

He heard Claire beside him, muttering something about reasons not to have dogs. Then she turned over, punched her pillow into the right shape and settled back down to sleep. Ben was sure he ought to be agreeing with her, but he had such a nice picture in his mind of Kyle and Tiger, on the floor together. If only his own problems were as simple to solve as that dog's.

If they were, it would be Claire's arm around him that would settle him down and make him stop whining. Now how could he accomplish that, since they'd grown so far apart lately? Nothing came instantly to mind. Ben folded his hands under his head and stared at the ceiling, pondering that problem and listening for peeper frogs in the dark.

* * *

There was cereal for breakfast, and fresh milk. But there were still no paper napkins. Claire hid her smile, watching her family use the last of the roll of paper towels. This could get interesting. She was probably the only one in the house who knew they had a supply of cloth napkins. She was also the only one who would know what to do with them, she reasoned.

Maybe Ben would surprise her. After all, he had surprised her big-time last night. He'd kept things under control with the puppy, insisting that the boys be the ones responsible for settling the dog down and getting up with him when necessary. Claire had actually slept most of the night, without dog interference.

Now she felt anxious to get a real start on The Caring Closet project. There wasn't a lot she could do before she saw at least one example of the work in progress. But donations were trickling in at church, and she could write the little speech she was going to need to make several times at various services Sunday. And there were probably a dozen lists to make regarding the project.

Lists, she could do. That was one of her strong points. Lists didn't even require dressing up and getting professional looking—just sitting at the kitchen table with a sharp pencil and a legal pad.

Of course, the moment she did that, Claire became a magnet for every male in the house, including Tiger.

"How much of this stuff do I put in here to prevent a repeat of yesterday's disaster?" Ben called over his shoulder while filling the dishwasher.

Kyle and Trent were involved in a squabble over the last clean pair of white socks. Tiger helped joyfully, trying to grab the socks out of their hands. To him, this tug of war was just another great game he wanted in on.

Claire looked around her kitchen at the confusion. In a matter of moments the volume had risen to where she couldn't hear herself think. "Just barely fill both those little containers. And close the top one after you fill it."

"That doesn't made any sense. Why fill it and then close it?" Ben muttered. Still, he did it, eyeing the dishwasher as if he expected it to spit an angry cascade of bubbles before he got it closed.

'And you two. Figure it out for yourselves without damage to the socks, your bodies or the furniture. And don't get that dog so excited, or you're going to have bigger problems than just the last pair of clean socks. Doesn't Dad have any in his drawer?"

"That's not fair!" Ben protested.

Both boys made sounds of disgust. "If he does,

they're those lame crew ones, anyway. Not the ankle-length ones like I wear.'' Trent made it clear what he thought of those.

"Then have Dad show you how to sort laundry and get a white load started, if his socks aren't good enough. I'll be out in Grandpa's apartment.'' And with that Claire picked up her pad and pencil to go make lists in the relative quiet of the rooms over the garage. They might be stuffy, and have very little furniture in them, but they were peaceful. And right now that was what counted.

Once in the apartment, Claire discovered other advantages. There was no "teenage'' music coming from an upstairs stereo. If Kyle and Trent were still arguing, she didn't know about it from across the driveway, making it very easy to start her work. And best of all, there was no telephone to ring and interrupt her. Of course, that also meant she couldn't make calls from the apartment, which was an inconvenience. But she could wait until her iced tea glass needed refilling to return to the house to use the phone.

She wondered if she could sneak the computer out here piece by piece. Maybe the boys wouldn't notice that their favorite indoor tool for games wasn't available, if she did it quickly while the summer was still new and the puppy required lots of attention.

With the computer out here, she could really make her father's empty apartment into Caring Closet headquarters. Looking around the nearly empty living room she could see the places where racks would fit around the walls. *Hangers,* she wrote down on her list of general supplies. A clothing store needed tons of hangers. And plastic bags—those large ones like the dry cleaner used, to keep the newly acquired outfits clean and presentable until they were needed for a job interview or other purpose.

And safety pins. Claire scribbled down items for her supplies list as fast as she could to keep up with her racing thoughts. The Caring Closet was taking shape under her fingers. And she had Ben and his awful dog to thank for the inspiration of moving out here. But she'd have to thank him later, much later.

If she went into the house now, she'd get involved with the dog or the kids, or doing laundry or seeing if the dishwasher was going to foam at the mouth again. Or, if Ben were still home, she'd get involved with thanking him for bringing in that awful dog. He looked anxious to be thanked in a very physical way for something, anything at all that he was doing. And while it would be fun, none of that would provide a growth experience for anyone.

Claire felt like adding a dozen roses to her supplies list, all for Gloria. Asking her father's new bride to be part of this project might be the single most important thing she had done so far. It definitely had inspired and organized her.

Claire kicked off her sandals and wiggled her toes. In her own house the slight griminess of the floor under her bare feet would have prompted her to leap up and clean instead of paying attention to the other work at hand. But she wasn't in her own house. She was in a space dedicated to The Caring Closet.

She had to remind herself to focus on planning the space and what was needed to fill it. No one was going to notice that the floor of this room where they met could use sweeping. "So I won't, either," she said out loud, happy to hear her voice ring in the empty space. If having a growth experience meant not cleaning, she could learn to enjoy this.

Chapter Eight

Claire had to be on her third outfit. This was quite unusual for her. Even though Ben was enjoying watching her change clothes, he felt bad for the indecision that was making her reject things from the closet.

"You're going to be fine. That looks good." He came up behind her, putting his arms around her waist. She felt wonderful and smelled even better. Burying his nose in her smooth hair made him aware of the shampoo she used. It also made him aware of how long it had been since he'd held her like this. Days, maybe even most of a week.

He expected her to push him away, fretful about everything that was going on for her. Instead, Claire relaxed into his arms. "Tell me more. I've missed hearing that kind of thing from you. I know you don't approve of this whole idea.''

''That's not true.'' His answer came out murmured, his face still close to her hair. ''I just don't want to see you get hurt, is all.'' It was difficult not to hold her even tighter, to protect her and shelter her from all the things out there that could hurt her.

He could feel her tense up as she answered.

''I won't get hurt. But I am nervous about this. And I think it's wonderful that you can handle the guys' doctor visits all by yourself. It takes such a load off my mind.'' She turned around, smiling up at him just inches from his face.

''Glad I could help out.'' His words sounded thick, a little slurred. It was looking into her eyes this close that made him tongue-tied. That always warmed his blood and slowed his tongue. He drew his wife even closer, to reassure her in the one way he knew how. She melted into his arms as he kissed her, and Ben wanted to stop time.

Apparently Claire had no such feelings, because in a moment she was drawing away. ''I won't look that good if we wrinkle this outfit.'' Frustration built in him, making him want to scowl. He tried to hold the feeling back for Claire's sake. She needed the reassurance, needed to be told she looked her best. But why did she have to look so kissable at the same time?

"At least I didn't smudge your makeup."

"No, but that only means I'm late putting it on. Don't forget to take that dog out before you leave with the kids," Claire admonished, businesslike again.

Well, that party was over. And stopping time was out of the question. Ben went back to his own search in the closet, wondering which shirt he could get away with not ironing for the ball game.

An hour later, Ben was ready to get up and pace the doctor's office. How long could it possibly take to get one kid checked out to play football? Ben looked at his watch again. This was ridiculous. They had been sitting in this waiting room for more than half an hour. Kyle had gone back into the depths of the medical office, gotten his allergy shot and come back to the waiting room in about ten minutes.

Since then, he and Kyle had waited for Trent. And waited some more. They had determined that there was no magazine newer than last year's Christmas guide to toys for preschoolers. Ben knew, because he'd looked through everything on every table, trying to distract himself from the wait.

Every whining, runny-nosed preschooler in Friedens was in this waiting room. Some of them were going to celebrate birthdays while they waited, apparently.

Finally Trent poked his head out of the doorway. "Dad? I need the form now."

Form? Ben had paid by check, and nobody had handed him any forms. "What form?" He knew he had to be looking at Trent as if the kid were speaking Swahili.

"The sports physical form. From the coach at school. That's why we're here, remember?" he said in that tone that only teenagers can adopt with their parents. Ben was surprised he passed up the eye roll to go with it.

"Yes, Trent. I remember all too well. But I figured you had the form. It's your physical. I didn't even go back there with you, remember?" Ben shot back in the same tone. He watched his son's eyes flash.

"I can't believe you didn't bring it. Mom would have. Now what am I going to do?"

Ben shrugged. "I guess you're going to bike back up here with the form once you find it at home. Or you're going to get your mom to take you back up here this afternoon. Because I'm already late for an appointment, and you need to hustle right now."

Trent looked as if he wanted to argue, then

thought better of it. He went back into the office and came out a few minutes later. "You don't have a stamp, do you?"

"No, I don't. I'm not in the habit of carrying stamps around in my pockets. And don't tell me your mother would have one."

Trent closed his mouth and scowled, heading out the front door of the doctor's office without another word.

"Come on. I need to get you guys home," Ben told Kyle, getting up and moving after Trent. Was this what life was like for Claire all the time? Of course not, because she knew how to handle the boys and was far more efficient around the house than Ben was ever going to be. Things for her went much smoother, he was sure.

This had to be about the tenth time this morning that one of the kids had reminded him, through words or a simple look, that he fell far short of perfect in the parent category. There had still been no paper napkins at breakfast, and now, thanks to mopping up after Tiger, they were out of paper towels.

The laundry was a disaster. How there could be that many white athletic socks in the dryer, but none of them a pair, was beyond him. And why did Kyle insist on wearing only some strange ones that had gaping holes in the feet? If Ben really tried to remember back that far, he could recall having favorite socks. But surely his hadn't looked like that. Of course not, because his father was never in charge of the laundry.

He didn't catch up to Trent until the parking lot, where his son lounged against the passenger side of the truck, trying to look nonchalant instead of locked out. That was the problem with being young and sulky. You lacked the power to really do anything—like storm into the vehicle when you didn't have a set of keys. Ben tried to keep his smile to himself.

A wave of empathy for his son swept over him. Instead of yelling at Trent, he felt like making things right between them. ''Look, I guess this is partly my fault. I'm not organized yet when it comes to stuff like filling out forms. And honestly, I thought you'd be bringing it yourself because it was important to you.'' He opened his own side of the truck and flipped the button for the passenger lock. Trent let Kyle elbow in past him to get the middle seat, then slid into the cab.

Trent stayed silent as he closed the door. ''Yeah, well. Maybe Mom will get me back up here with the form when she gets home later. I really need it filled out, that exact form, before they'll let me start practice.''

''Then one way or another we'll make sure that

happens. I know this is important to you." Ben started the truck to head for home. He didn't run any stop signs on the way, but he cut every other corner that he could, dropping the guys off at the house in record time.

Even with all the rushing he'd done, he'd be lucky to get to the stadium before the national anthem. He hoped Marcy would be patient, waiting in front of Stan Musial's statue for him the way they had planned. The kids were waving in his rearview mirror, and he waved back as he planned the quickest way to downtown St. Louis. How fast could he go on the interstate without catching the attention of the highway patrol? He was about to find out.

Why was she nervous? And feeling so intimidated? Claire could feel her palms sweating. She felt as if this were a job interview, or the first day of school—and it wasn't pleasant.

She thought back to this morning, when Ben had tried his best to put her at ease. It was so hard not to stay there, where she felt safe in his arms. Why did the man have to be right so often? And how did he know what she needed so instinctively, yet drive her crazy at the same time?

Here at the church, Nessa was doing all she could to calm her. The young woman was friendly and pleasant, showing Claire all the facets of the ministry in the large church in Union. But even her casual questions about what Claire had done already about receiving clothing, and what systems they had in place for client intake, made Claire nervous.

It pointed out just how far she had to go to get this project up and running. Maybe Ben and the Grump Sisters and all her other detractors were right. Maybe she had absolutely no business doing this. Looking around at the organized room Nessa was showing her made Claire sure of it. Whoever had put this together knew what they were doing, and it showed. Any attempt to do the same with her few volunteers at Friedens Chapel was likely to be a disaster.

"Claire? Hello?" Nessa put a hand on her arm, bringing Claire out of her panicky reverie. "How about that glass of iced tea with Ann now? You look like you could use it."

"You have no idea." Claire looked around for Ann, who was the project leader at this church. She didn't see anyone who fit her mental image of the organized soul who had put this all together. Like Nessa, she'd be young and svelte and wearing a suit like the ones they took in for clients, Claire thought. Her hair would be perfect and her nails freshly done.

But the only people in the room were two workers sorting clothing out of a box. Both women were well past forty. They wore no-nonsense cotton shirts and pants that looked as if they might be polyester. Running shoes completed their outfits, and there wasn't any nail polish between them. As Claire pondered all that, the woman with mostly silver hair swept back in a ponytail straightened up from what she was doing.

"Did I hear my name?" She had a pleasant smile and sparkling blue eyes. Dusting off a hand on her navy-blue pant leg, she turned to Claire. "I'm Ann. And we have iced tea in the fridge in the office, if you're ready. On a day like this one, I'm always ready for a chance to sit and talk."

Claire took her hand. Surprise and relief fought in her. This was an ordinary person, a wife and mother just like Claire. And she'd done wonderful things in this church to provide for people with this ministry. Maybe Claire was worrying too much. Maybe God would use her and the others around her at Friedens Chapel to build something every bit as wonderful.

"I'd love some tea," she said. "And lots of advice on the side."

"Claire's still new at this," Nessa piped up. "Maybe you can put her mind at ease that it can be done without the combined talents of Donald Trump and Martha Stewart.''

They all laughed at that, and Claire felt more of the burden lifted off her shoulders. Ann had a nice laugh and a good handshake. She felt like a friend, even though Claire didn't know anything else about her. It gave Claire more hope than she'd had in quite some time.

An hour flashed by over iced tea. Claire stared at the nearly empty pitcher and then looked at her watch. She had several pages of legal pad filled with new notes, and Ann and her fellow worker had taken turns giggling at her earnest scribbling of their bits of advice. Sitting down to tea with Nessa had helped, too. It was nice to see that the polished young woman had the same concerns Claire and the others faced, like dealing with squabbling kids and pushy church committee members.

"This has been the most wonderful morning," Claire told the other women at the table. "You have no idea how much more comfortable I feel about this whole project now."

Ann laughed again. "Great. If hearing about our mistakes and blunders does somebody good, then maybe they were all worthwhile."

"I have to admit I'm relieved myself." Nessa stood and picked up her empty glass. "Until this morning, I wasn't sure if you were the right person to do this or not, Claire.''

"My incompetence showed, huh?'' Claire stood up with her and picked up her notes.

Nessa shook her head. "Just the opposite. You seemed so together and organized that I wasn't sure you had the compassion to do the job. The organizational skills are great—they make the job a whole bunch easier, I'm told.'' Nessa waved a hand. "Since I've had to learn them the hard way, I'm always envious of folks who seem to have been born with them. But the caring part of The Caring Closet is what I can't teach you. Until I saw that you were just as human as the rest of us this morning, I wasn't sure if the ministry at Friedens was going to work.''

Claire felt like throwing her head back and laughing. Nessa thought she looked calm and organized? She must be doing a great job of hiding her insecurity. "I have to go home and make a long distance call to tell my sister this. She'll tease me for days after I tell her how worried I was, and what you said.'' Claire knew Laurel would also remind her of just what she'd forgotten until now: that when they let God be the one in control of the situation, the outcome was always good.

The drive home to Friedens seemed much quicker than the trip to Union had this morning.

Claire wondered what the guys had done about lunch. If she weren't sure they had already taken apart the kitchen making sandwiches or frozen pizza, she would go through the drive-thru at their favorite burger joint and bring home a treat.

However, it was nearly one, and they'd probably eaten an hour ago or more. She bypassed the fast-food places and went straight home, even pushing away the temptation to stop at the grocery store and pick up paper napkins and a few ripe vegetables for dinner.

When she got home, she was surprised to see the guys on the driveway shooting hoops. It was a fairly warm day, and she had figured they'd be inside, or at least that the dog would be out with them. They ran up to the car before she even got the engine turned off, motioning for her to open the door.

"Keys, Mom. We need your keys. Like, right now." Kyle sounded urgent. "Tiger's been in there for hours."

"Why didn't you let him out, then?" Claire tried not to lecture about the consequences of neglecting the puppy. They'd be the ones cleaning up after him, anyway.

"Because Dad dropped us off in a hurry." Trent's voice was angry.

"Yeah, and he didn't stop when we tried to get

him to, and neither of us had our keys. So we've been out here playing basketball and drinking water out of the hose, and Tiger's been inside scratching at the door.'' Kyle looked even more distressed than he sounded.

"Great." Claire hurried to the door. "I hate to think what that kitchen looks like." She didn't have to wait long to find out. The moment the door was open, Tiger bowled out and down the steps, thrilled to see human company.

Claire stood one step inside the kitchen door, trying not to shriek. The forty-pound bag of puppy kibble had been torn open and crunched underfoot. The metal mixing bowl that had apparently held the dog's water was upside down over a spreading puddle. One kitchen chair was knocked over, and huge paw prints marked the table and countertop where Tiger had explored after knocking down his baby gate. And this was just the kitchen. Claire could only imagine what the rest of the house looked like. How far had this beast gotten?

"Oh, wow." Kyle sounded in awe of the mess before him. "It's going to take the rest of the day for us to clean this up."

It was then that Claire's control snapped. When she closed her eyes to try and calm down, a red haze covered her field of vision. This was all Ben's fault, and this time she wasn't cleaning up after him. It might mean more work for the boys until Ben got home, but they weren't entirely blameless in this situation.

"It may take you longer than that," Claire told him and his equally unhappy brother. "Because as of right now I am out of here. Gone. I'm moving to Grandpa's old apartment where things are peaceful. You four males are officially on your own for the duration."

Chapter Nine

$\sim$

"**Y**ou're kidding, right?" Trent sounded as if he couldn't believe what his mother was saying. This had to be a joke. He looked more like the little boy she remembered from just a few short years ago, whose hair and feelings both got rumpled much more easily than they did today.

It hurt a little to disillusion him. But Claire felt she had to. Her own feelings got hurt often enough, and she survived. She felt pretty wounded right now, thanks to Ben's thoughtlessness.

"No, Trent, I'm not kidding. The Caring Closet project at church is very important to me. I've tried to make your dad aware of just how important it is that I do this, and do a good job of it. But he doesn't seem to be catching on. If I stay in the house and do my normal stuff, along with cleaning up after dog disasters like this one, I won't accomplish anything else. And this time I'm determined to get other things done.''

"Why?'' Kyle joined the argument. He had his chin thrust out in an effort to look tough, Claire suspected. That way he wouldn't give away anything. She could still detect a faint tremble in his lower lip. Not that she would let him know that she noticed, of course. Let him keep what little dignity he had left. Of course, there was also the fact that if Trent discovered that his brother was so upset, he'd tease him about it, and World War Three would erupt before she could even think about moving things out to her father's tranquil apartment.

She still hadn't answered Kyle's question, and he wasn't going to let things go. "Aren't we more important than that dumb Closet thing?''

Claire had the greatest temptation to give up on all of this and just hug her baby. But he was eleven, and Gloria's reminder to use all this for growth, for everybody, was coming back again. So she just put a hand on his shoulder. Under her fingers she could feel the tense muscles his anger produced. "You will always be more important than anything else I take on, especially a project to help others at church. I couldn't very well minister to somebody else without my own house in order, could I?'' This didn't seem to be the answer Kyle expected. His stance eased a little, shoulders relaxing.

"Okay. But I still don't see why you have to leave."

"It's not like I'm going far. I'll be across the driveway. And you can always bother me if it's something important. I'm just not going to follow around behind you guys and that dog with a mop and broom right now, sweeping up the disasters he created. Got it?''

Both boys sighed. "Yeah, we got it. Let's get some of this cleaned up before he makes more of a mess," Trent said. "Kyle, you take him outside, and I'll make lunch. What do you want on your sandwich?''

"Everything. I'm starved. Where's the leash?''

So a crisis was averted. Claire watched them work together for a moment. That did her heart good. If it weren't for really needing Ben to see how serious she was about getting this project off to a good, solid start, she wouldn't be tempted to move out to the apartment. But her sweet, thick-headed husband wasn't going to catch on any other way.

She went upstairs to find a suitcase. This was an operation that called for packing so she wouldn't have to break her resolve and come back to the house on an hourly basis.

Upstairs she found her seldom-used suitcase and began to ponder what to put into it. She'd need all her notes and paperwork on the project. And she'd need cosmetics, a couple of changes of clothing and basic toiletries. If Ben didn't catch on right away, he'd figure out what was going on once he noticed that her toothbrush and her pillow were missing. Of course, given Ben's normal sensitivity, that might take a while.

She could hear the sounds of furniture being put right while she packed. Trent had the kitchen radio on at a volume that made her ears ring. Claire wondered if Tiger would howl. Once he came in and heard that racket, he'd want to. That provided another reason for her to pack quickly and get out of here.

Ben started scouting for Marcy when he was still on the footbridge between the parking garage and the stadium property. He could see her from about a block away. Marcy wasn't patient. She also didn't know how to dress for ball games. Or she had decided that business was more important than comfort. Ben felt out of place in his Cardinal-red golf shirt and khakis, even though he was still more dressed up than most of the fans who were inside Busch Stadium.

Compared to Marcy, he looked like a slob. He couldn't imagine her making it up to the box seats in those heels she had on, or that extremely narrow black skirt. And who wore a jacket, even a linen one, to a ball game? He had to admit she looked nice, but she looked massively overdressed. While he hadn't expected Marcy to show up in the middle of the business day in shorts, a suit seemed too restricting in the midday St. Louis heat.

Taking Claire to the ball game was always fun, he thought. She usually wore those red shorts he liked so much, and looked like a million dollars in them.

"Hey," he said as he drew close to the statue where Marcy stood in the little shade that she could find. "You look nice." She did look nice. "Sorry I'm late."

She waved a hand at him, dismissing his apology. At least her nails were lacquered in Cardinal red.

"You're not late. I just get every place a little early." At least she was tactful. But then, since she was the one trying to buy his family business, she had a vested interest in being tactful.

"So, where is this box, anyway? Anywhere I can get a good fly ball?"

Marcy shook her head. Funny, she didn't look all that attractive doing it. When Claire shook her head, her soft hair flowed in waves and actually bounced a little. Marcy's shorter, much more controlled hairstyle just moved with her like a helmet. "Afraid not. Real good sight lines, but no foul balls, usually. Even from the power hitters. You'll just have to buy the guys T-shirts or something."

Ben shrugged. "Not quite the same. Although I might get T-shirts just to stretch the clean laundry for a few more days."

"Claire that busy? I thought she didn't work." Marcy's sidelong glance as they walked in through the turnstile at the stadium entrance made him cautious. She didn't sound as if she approved.

Ben laughed, wondering how much of this crazy mess he ought to explain to Marcy. Probably the less said the better. "I should tell you it's all your fault." That would put her on the defensive.

"Oh?" Her raised eyebrow was a perfect arch. Maybe too perfect. Coy looks had never been appealing to him.

"Yeah, all the hush-hush secrecy about this business deal has me in the doghouse. Can you believe she even brought up some fable about how half the senior class thought you and I were an item in high school?"

Marcy went quickly from coy to flustered. Ben

almost regretted what he'd said when he saw her face flush.

"Really? How…odd." She faltered for a minute, covering a misstep by looking down at the tickets. Ben found that a little strange. Surely she knew where her own company box was. "I don't think I'd heard that one before. But I am glad you're keeping this quiet. If word got out around town that we were interested in your property, things could get touchy."

"Hey, this is Claire we're talking about, not the town crier or something. Anyway, she's too busy setting up some mission thing at church to be worried about what I'm doing right now."

Marcy's red lips formed an O of sympathy. "That's too bad. Is that really why you're out of clean T-shirts?"

"That about covers it." No sense in telling her the whole story. This way he looked slightly neglected. The truth would probably make him look arrogant and not terribly bright. And those weren't the qualities to project when one was trying to sell the family business. He looked at the concession stands. "So, are we stopping for hot dogs?"

"No need to stop. We can call from the box. The courtesy phone brings somebody from food service."

This wasn't what he was used to. A courtesy

phone meant uniformed ushers that looked more like security guards who stood at the doors, letting in the patrons.

So they'd be watching baseball from air-conditioned comfort? Somehow it didn't seem quite right. But for one afternoon he could tolerate it. Especially when Marcy's company was footing the bill.

Besides, if he had a nice lunch in the cool comfort of the box, he'd feel less stressed. And ready to take on that mountain of chores at home and the equally huge mountain of store paperwork piling up in Friedens when he got back tonight. Maybe he could even convince the guys that take-out Chinese would be as good as home-cooked burgers. He knew you could get disposable forks and chopsticks with take-out. Did Chinese food come with its own paper napkins? It was worth finding out.

By five in the evening, Claire's resolve to stay in her dad's apartment was wearing thin. True, she'd arranged everything to her satisfaction. But she definitely needed a phone to do all her committee business. And she felt a little bad about abandoning the boys to their dog cleanup and training. She was so used to taking care of everybody that it felt strange *not* to do it.

But if she caved now, Ben won. That was the only thing keeping her out here.

She wondered what the guys were going to have for dinner. Burgers on the grill, if Ben got home in time, probably. It was the star of his cooking repertoire. In fact, it was the only thing in his repertoire.

When the phone at her elbow rang, Claire jumped. She picked it up. "Hello?"

"Hey, kid. My grandsons told me you were hiding out in my old place."

Her dad sounded more cheerful than worried, but Claire knew he was digging for information.

"What's up?" he asked.

"Nothing serious. Did they tell you about your new grand-dog? He's mostly the reason I'm out here."

"He sounded a little boisterous when I was on the phone with Kyle."

Claire could hear the smile in her father's voice. "Boisterous is kind. He's a monster, but he's just a pup, so maybe he'll outgrow some of his bad behavior. I hope so, because he's going to be the size of a tank." The picture of Tiger full grown with the enthusiasm he already displayed made her shudder. "I didn't think this phone still worked. Thought you had it disconnected and your calls forwarded to Gloria's number."

"I meant to. Hadn't gotten around to doing it, but it sounds like that will come in handy. You can't do business there without a phone. Besides, if you're really intent on staying out there, it isn't safe without one."

Now he sounded like Sheriff Dad. "I know. But I'm fine, really. And I won't be staying here alone that much. Once we get this project off the ground, I'll move back into the house. Just don't tell Ben that."

"You two on the outs?"

That sounded like her dad, too. Always got to the point.

"If there's anything I can do, believe me—"

"No, Dad, really. We are not 'on the outs,' as you so charmingly put it. Just having a discussion about what my job is supposed to be around here. And what his job is, for that matter. This just struck me as the best way to make my point."

"Like he could miss one of your points on something."

Even on the phone, Claire could visualize her dad's teasing grin.

"Don't stay out there too long. It can't be all that comfortable. I didn't leave that much in the place."

"That suits me just fine. More room for the racks of clothes we'll be collecting." Claire was struck with one bit of inspiration. "You didn't happen to leave any paper napkins in the pantry, did you? Those, I could use."

Dad sounded confused. "Probably. I always keep a big old package on hand because I never remember to buy them and that way I don't run out too often. Why is it you women set such store by that kind of stuff? Gloria has a second pantry down in the basement, and I swear half of it is paper towels and fancy napkins and such. She wouldn't run out of anything like that if we entertained the whole Sheriff's Department." He sounded amused and proud at the same time. Married life was obviously agreeing with him.

"Good. It will get you used to being civilized again. And thanks for worrying about me even when you didn't need to. Can I ask you to keep the phone connected, and I'll reimburse you at the end of the month?"

"I'll keep it connected. But don't worry about the bill. Think of it as my contribution to this Caring Closet thing. That and the emptying of my wife's closets as donations, I understand…"

Claire had to smile. "I didn't ever suggest she empty the whole closet. Besides, you needed more room for your stuff, didn't you?"

"Huh. I think I brought three uniforms, two pairs of shoes, one church suit and two sets of fishing clothes with me, all told. That doesn't exactly fill up much closet space. Do you know how many pairs of black shoes alone this woman has?''

This could be a long conversation. But at least Dad wasn't worried about his little girl anymore. ''Does that include boots?'' she teased him.

About six-thirty, there was pounding on the downstairs door. Claire went down and looked out the peephole, knowing who she would find. When she opened the door, Ben almost fell over from the force of his continued knocking.

He straightened himself up. His dark eyes were flashing, and he glowered. ''You can't do this.''

His ultimatum put her on the defensive from the beginning. ''I already did.''

''Then come back. Now.''

''I don't think so. Definitely not when you're using that tone of voice.''

''Look, you can't just walk out over, what, a little mess? Made by the dog, I might add, not me and the kids.''

''The dog wouldn't have made the mess if you'd been doing your job as a parent. What was so important that you couldn't come in with the kids instead of leaving them at the curb?''

Ben bristled. ''I didn't leave them at the curb, exactly. And I told you I had an important meeting in St. Louis.''

"With Marcy?" She had to ask, even though she knew the answer.

"With Marcy." Ben deflated a little, looking less like a warrior. "Now if that's settled, will you come back to the house?"

"Sort of."

She could see his face flush in another rush of anger. "Sort of? What's that supposed to mean?"

Claire looked down at the floor. She'd been wrestling with this part and she didn't know what to do. "I'll come in to eat dinner. I don't want the boys more upset than they already are."

Ben scowled. "Great. Let's not upset the kids. Me, it's okay to upset. But not your precious kids."

"You know I didn't mean it that way." Claire wanted to reach out and touch him to reassure him, but at the same time that felt wrong. Because she couldn't give him all the reassurance he wanted.

"Then how did you mean it?" Ben's eyes bored into her, challenging her and making her squirm. "And does that mean you're coming back or not?"

"I don't know. Are you ready to tell me more about your business with Marcy?" That wasn't what she meant to say. But deep down it was what she felt, and Claire wasn't going to apologize for it, either.

"No. I've already told you everything you need to know."

How could he be so stubborn? Claire wanted to pound the wall next to her. "Ben, that isn't good enough. You're the one who started reminding me about marriage vows just last week. And I'm pretty sure honesty figures prominently in those vows. You can't shut me out of your decisions like this and expect me to be happy."

Now Ben was the one looking at the floor. "When I'm ready to tell you what's going on, I will. I promise you'll be the first to know. But Claire, I can't tell you now. Just take my word that it's business and I'm doing what's best for all of us."

"That's not good enough. When you're ready to share more than that, I'll be back to the house. Until then, I have plenty to keep me busy out here."

Claire began to close the door, and Ben blocked it with one straightened arm. "Oh, no. We're not going to end this discussion that way." He looked angry now, angrier than Claire had ever seen him. "I could just pick you up and carry you back there. I'm man enough, you know."

"Do it and it will be the last time you ever touch me. That's never been the way our relationship has worked before, and it isn't going to start now."

"Then what can I do to please you?" he barked.

"For starters you could tell me the truth. All of it, right now. That would take more effort than carrying me across the yard, wouldn't it?"

When he looked at her, Claire could hardly keep from crying. She hadn't meant to hurt Ben like this, but there was no going back now. Ben didn't say anything else, but his look told her everything she needed to know.

"I guess I got my answer. I'll be over in ten minutes to eat dinner. I'll walk over on my own. And when I'm done, I'll be walking right back here." The door slammed with more force than she'd intended.

Claire leaned against it, aware that she was trembling. She hadn't intended to get this angry. She hadn't expected to see Ben this upset. This was becoming much bigger than she'd planned.

The battle lines had been drawn.

Chapter Ten

Sunday after church, Claire went to the row of cubbyholes where every family at church had a mailbox. She'd added The Caring Closet designation to their mailbox, and was now happy to see it was even fuller than usual.

She took out the sheaf of notes, flyers about activities and other papers, and sorted through them. There were a few things for each of the boys, and one flyer about fall sports leagues that was addressed to Ben. Otherwise, the bulk of the mail seemed to be Caring Closet stuff. This was beginning to feel like a real ministry.

She'd had the staff print up a little notice about the project to include in the Sunday bulletin. It was rather cute, she thought, especially where she'd used the little graphic that looked like a suggestion box for questions and comments.

Flipping through the responses was encouraging. Several asked about donations and specific needs. Two others were already anxious to know how referrals to the program would work. But about halfway down, Claire found a slip; as she read it her fingers grew cold and her face numb.

Go back to paying more attention to your family. Maybe then your husband won't have to run around St. Louis with strange women.

How incredibly ugly! Claire's first thought was to crush the slip into a ball and throw it away on the spot.

Instead, she buried it in the bottom of the pile and went to her Sunday school class. She got there as the roll was being taken. Ben had saved her a seat. When she slid into it, he looked up.

"What's wrong?"

She must look as shaky as she felt. "Nothing," she lied. This wasn't the place to discuss the nasty little note she'd gotten. Somehow she plowed through the lesson, even though she contributed next to nothing. When class was over and the halls of the education building were filled with milling families, Claire could only look at all the faces.

Who had sent her this note? And how seriously should she take such a mean-spirited act?

Tuesday morning, Claire paced the apartment waiting for her committee members to get there. When the bell rang the first time, she went downstairs to face Patsy and Peggy. Her shoulders drooped. Why couldn't Gloria be first so that they could talk?

Still the good hostess, she started to welcome them in, but Peggy interrupted her. "You may not want us here after Patsy tells you something." She almost pushed her sister through the door. "I'd like to apologize for her in advance."

"It seemed like a good idea at the time," Patsy muttered.

Something about the look on her face told Claire what Patsy was about to say.

"I found a note in my mailbox at church. Do you know what that was about?"

Patsy grimaced. "I'm afraid I do. And my sister has convinced me that in this day and age, two adults going to a baseball game together is more likely a business meeting than a tryst."

"So you saw Ben at a ball game with someone?" Claire felt relieved and aggravated at the same time. Relieved that this had all been over a ball game, but aggravated that she hadn't known about the outing in advance.

Patsy nodded. "With Marcy McKinnon. Who still uses too much makeup, in my opinion." Spoken like a true high school teacher. Claire kept the grin off her face.

Of course, it had to be Marcy. "Ben is doing business with her company."

Patsy sniffed. "That wouldn't be the business I'd worry about. Did you know she's divorced?"

"No, it hadn't come up." Ben hadn't said anything about Marcy's marital status. He might not even know himself. Claire looked back at Patsy. "Can we put this behind us and go back to business? And can I assume that anything else you see, you'll talk to me about in person?"

"Of course. And I'm sorry for overreacting—"

Before Patsy could say anything else, Gloria stepped in the still-open doorway behind the sisters. "Looks like I missed something momentous," she said, coming to the heart of the matter with uncanny accuracy.

"Come and get some iced tea, and we'll all talk," Claire said. "I don't know if we're ever going to get to real committee business today."

Gloria waved a hand in dismissal. "We can't do much real business with four of us, and most of the rest are usually late, anyway. Let's go."

It was Peggy who looked around the apartment while they sat and sipped tea, and asked the fateful question. "Are you living out here? This looks like more than just committee stuff."

Claire nodded. "I guess I am. I hadn't intended to. It just turned out that way." She told them the condensed version of her arguments with Ben, and the mess Tiger had made of the house.

Gloria made sympathetic noises and poured iced tea, and all three women listened. "Why do I feel I caused some of this?" Gloria asked with a wry expression. "When I was talking about growth experiences, I'm not sure this is what I had in mind."

"Hey, I'm nothing if not enthusiastic. Give me an idea to take hold of, and I do just that." Claire picked up her tea glass, rattled the ice, set it back down again. "I'm just worried that I've taken hold of this one too much."

"And that note couldn't have helped," Peggy said pointedly, looking at her sister.

Patsy covered her face. "All right. Okay. If you'd come along with the Golden Agers on the bus, you could have straightened me out then and there."

Claire shook her head. "Let's stop worrying about that part. Right now I feel like The Caring Closet is on track, and I'm doing real well with that. We've got so much stuff gathered and we're almost ready to set up shop. But at the same time my personal life is falling apart.''

Gloria spoke up. ''Is it falling apart, or just taking a new direction? Not all change is bad. And it sounds like you're due for one. Maybe there's more of God's hand in this than you know.''

''Maybe. I'm just not sure.'' Claire tried not to wring her hands. She felt so jumpy, so baffled by everything.

Gloria was still there and still listening. ''I'm pretty new at this faith stuff. It's taken all kinds of crises in my own life to make talking to God more natural again. I guess I have my daughter-in-law to thank for that. And I know what she'd ask you right now, so pardon me if I sound like Lori. Do you want to pray about it?''

''Yes.'' They joined hands over the coffee table while the other women silently bowed their heads. Holding on to Gloria felt like a lifeline. Claire began, faltering at first. ''Father, I feel lost. I think I'm doing Your will in all this and I know this is a job that You want me to do. But I'm so confused. Did I do the right thing moving out here? I miss Ben and the kids.'' She paused to collect her thoughts. Gloria squeezed her hands, and in the warm silence Claire could hear the noise of several sets of feet coming up the stairs. ''Just guide me through this. Lead me the way You want me to go. Amen."

Claire felt more at peace than she had in days. "Thanks. I needed that." She looked at the older woman. "Now I need one more thing."

"Give it a shot, and I'll try my best."

Claire took a deep breath. "What am I supposed to call you? I know you're my stepmother now, but I'm not ready to call you 'Mom'."

"You may never be ready for that."

Gloria's words were practical, with no touch of hurt. That made her glad, because she didn't want to hurt Gloria, just figure out their relationship.

"You had a mother and I won't try to take her place. Let's just stick with first names for now. If something else feels right later, we can work on it." She gave Claire a quick hug.

"Fine with me." Before Claire could say anything else, the living room was full of people who'd arrived all at once. The committee work began as soon as she got everybody settled.

Things went smoothly, or at least as smoothly as could be expected, for quite a while. They sorted garments, put donations into piles that might need a little mending, dry cleaning or other touch-up work. There were a few things that were in perfect condition, and those were exclaimed over and put on nice hangers. The rack in the corner that held clothing ready to be worn began to fill up.

Linda had been looking over a pile of blouses for missing buttons or any other problems, when she looked up. "Do we need any extra hands on the committee?"

"Probably. Why?" Claire asked, still going through index cards and noting possible outfit combinations.

"My cousin Marcy may be moving back to town. And I figure that after her rough divorce, she needs plenty to keep herself busy. Although something about her job must be working because she sounded a lot more cheerful last night when I talked to her on the phone."

Linda didn't notice the general silence that fell over the room. Claire noticed Peggy and Patsy exchange glances. Before Linda could say anything else, Kyle thundered up the stairs and into the room. For once Claire wanted to kiss him for interrupting.

Seeing so many women working gave him a moment's pause. "Sorry, Mom. I know I shouldn't interrupt you. But I need to ask you something important. Hi, Grandma Gloria. Hi, everybody." At least he hadn't lost his manners totally. And Claire knew the 'Grandma Gloria' part would win him points with every lady in the room, especially his new grandmother.

"What is it, Kyle?"

"Are we allergic to dogs? Is that why we haven't had one before?"

"Not that I know of. Why, are you and Trent sneezing? Are your eyes itchy?"

Kyle shook his head. "Nope. Not that. But remember when I had that ear infection once, and you gave me the medicine and I broke out in bumps?"

"I sure do. Hives. Bright pink and all over."

Kyle's eyes lit up; he looked happy to be understood. He also seemed to be unable to stand still. He lifted one foot off the floor and rubbed one battered tennis shoe against the other bony ankle. "Right. Anyway, I think we all have those bumps. And they keep getting worse when we're around Tiger." All the time he spoke, he kept rubbing that ankle.

"Bumps. And they're red and itchy? Do you have them everywhere?" Gloria seemed to fight back giggles when Kyle nodded. What did she know that Claire didn't?

"Not all over. Mostly on our legs. Where Tiger rubs up against us, I guess. That's why I wondered if we're allergic to him. That would be awful, giving up the dog because we're allergic to him."

Kyle's expression told them all what a heartbreak that would be.

Gloria motioned to him. "Come over here and let me look at your so-called hives. I have an idea what they might be. And if I'm right, your mom might let you keep the dog. After you give him a couple of baths, that is."

Realization dawned on Claire as Gloria peered down at the boy's ankles. They were red and bumpy, and itched furiously, judging from the way Kyle was still rubbing.

Red itchy bumps around the ankles. And everybody in the house had them, brought on by contact with the dog. "Oh, no. Fleas! Kyle, those are flea bites!" There was a bit of panic in her voice.

Everybody else must have caught on about the same time she did. If this had been happening to somebody else, it would have been funny. The looks of the others, ranging from squeamish to horrified, were priceless. Gloria shrugged. She was the only one who didn't look fazed by the situation. But then, Claire remembered, she was also the only one in the room who had a herd of goats to deal with at home. They probably presented her with more challenging pests than fleas.

The room erupted in conversation again. Claire could hear various soaps and potions being discussed, and the virtues of boiling cloth items versus using boric acid. "No, that's for roaches," she heard Peggy say. Naturally, Patsy was contradicting.

How lovely. Not only did she have a fifty-pound puppy that wasn't fully house-trained, but she now had a house full of fleas. *Ugh.* That helped make up her mind about going back there to sleep for a while. The very thought made her skin crawl. Fleas! Claire couldn't help but rub her bare ankles as hard as Kyle was rubbing his.

At six, Ben was at the door to the apartment. He seemed a little gruff when Claire came down to talk to him. "I'm grilling burgers. Do you want to eat with us? And can I come in while they cook?"

Claire looked him up and down. "If you take off those shoes at the door. Thank you for changing into shorts."

"Hey, I remember a few things from my scouting days." Ben smiled as he eased into the hallway, slipping off his shoes. "And I brought home everything from the store that the guys said we needed to start fighting the fleas."

Claire shivered. The thought of those little things jumping around all over her house... "Thank you. I don't even have to remind you that this wouldn't have been necessary—"

"If I hadn't shown the poor judgment of getting

the dog in the first place? You're right. It was a lousy idea. You want to tell Kyle that? I sure don't."

Claire grimaced. "You know I'm as soft as you are when it comes to the kids. Tiger's already been here too long to give him up. I have to admit, it was almost cute watching the guys give the big lug a bath in that washtub in the backyard. Did you know that Trent even warmed the water first? He didn't want his big baby to catch a chill."

Ben shrugged. "Hey, Tiger doesn't have a lot of fur. He could catch cold or something, as sleek as he is."

"Ben, it's July. He won't catch cold unless somebody stuffs him in the refrigerator."

"I don't think he'd fit. He's already grown, I swear. You would have known just by looking at him that he's going to be a moose, wouldn't you? Another one of my brilliant moves. Not only do I get a dog, but I get one with fleas, who is going to be the size of my truck when he's full grown."

He looked defeated. The lines around his eyes were back, and his shoulders slumped. Claire gave in to the urge to wrap her arms around him. She wasn't sure if she was seeking comfort or giving it, or maybe a little of both.

The moment she hugged him, she regretted it. Ben felt great and smelled even better: sharp, spicy aftershave mingled with a light aura of woodsmoke. It was a heady combination, especially when she had been deprived of her husband's company for a few days. "Mmm." She couldn't help murmuring and burying her nose into the crisp cotton of his shirt. "You smell good."

"You smell even better." His voice was low and husky. "What would you say to a truce? I really miss you." Claire could feel him nuzzling her hair, and it nearly made her lose what little resolve she still had.

"I miss you, too. But there's still a lot of work to do on The Caring Closet. And you are so distracting." As if to prove her point, Ben was running his hands up and down her back. If he were any more distracting, she wouldn't be able to frame words that made sense.

Then his hands stopped in the middle of her back, and that was even more maddening than the movement. All she could do was lean into his welcoming body and feel his embrace. There was no doubt in her mind that this was where she belonged.

He lowered his head and kissed her. When their lips met, Claire tingled with warmth. His hands tightened around her back, and Claire knew that her grasp on Ben's neck was intense. She could feel his muscles jump under her fingers, his mouth slanted over hers.

When she was breathless, he pulled back for a moment. "You think the guys would notice if dinner was a little late?" Ben's breath was hot on her ear, and she shivered at the sensation.

She had to be the one to control this situation. And she was perilously close to losing her control. She took a deep breath, not surprised that it came out a little shuddery. She'd prayed that God would show her what to do earlier. Now she was more confused than ever.

That was hard for Claire to imagine. Surely flinging themselves at each other wasn't what God had in mind. She tried to look serious. "We can't just delay dinner. They'd notice. Which is why we need to keep any truce talks limited to daylight hours, standing up. Preferably separated by more distance than this. There's still plenty separating us that won't be helped by this kind of behavior." Claire backed out of his embrace reluctantly.

The things they needed to settle required talking to each other. Working with each other. They didn't need to act like teenagers just because they'd been apart a few days. There was no doubt in her mind that the physical part of their relationship still worked. It was the mental and emotional partnership that needed attention.

"Spoilsport," he muttered. "But you never answered my question. Will you eat with us?"

"Sure. Why don't we eat out on the picnic table when you're ready? It's not too hot tonight for that, and we can put the silly dog out on a tie-out and have him roll in the grass. Maybe it will knock off some of those pesky fleas."

"What a lovely picture." Ben grimaced. "But it would be easier than getting the guys to set the table inside. Kind of like a picnic."

"That sounds nice. And I think it might be best if I sat at the picnic table and watched you grill, instead of both of us coming back in here."

Ben sighed. "Man, you really are a spoilsport. But you're probably right. You were always the one with sense when we were dating. That hasn't changed, has it? I'll get the grill going, get the meat and start cooking."

He started toward the house, Claire watching him from the doorway. A few steps down the path, he turned. "Guess I need my shoes."

She couldn't help giggling. "Guess you do." She watched him come back and slip into his shoes, then head toward the house again.

"Like I said, you're the one with sense. But not all the sense. Just wait until you see what I picked up on the way home to complete dinner."

Claire watched him go to start the fire, whistling

as he went. If any other man had said that, she would have expected fine French wine, maybe, or a bouquet of flowers in just the right vase. But she knew what Ben Jericho needed to complete dinner tonight. Paper napkins.

Maybe he was learning, after all.

Chapter Eleven

Dinner around the picnic table was as enjoyable as any date Claire had ever had. Of course the company was good, and the guys all seemed to be on best behavior. Even Tiger, lolling on his tie-out chain, wasn't begging too much. He also wasn't scratching much, either, which was a good thing. Maybe that bath the guys gave him was working.

Ben had grilled burgers just right, and the boys had taken care of the condiments. Things may have been served on plastic plates, but there was fresh lettuce and garden tomatoes, and plenty of paper napkins. Trent even surprised her by showing that he knew how to fix corn on the cob.

He made light of his efforts. ''Mom, it's just

boiling water. Shucking the things was the hardest part.''

''No, keeping Tiger out of the corn shucks was the hardest part,'' Kyle grumbled. ''Why would even a dog want to eat corn silk?''

''Hey, it must have looked interesting to him. I'm glad you're not letting him eat things that aren't good for him, though. I'll bet that is a full-time job.''

Kyle nodded. ''Was I this much trouble? Because if I was, I'm surprised you kept me.''

Ben laughed. ''You weren't this much trouble all the time. Not like this dog. And you had a great smile, which softened everybody up so they weren't mad at you too often.''

''Yeah, only when you flushed something important down the toilet.'' Trent was grinning now. Kyle buried his head in his arms in response. Claire couldn't tell if he was laughing or embarrassed.

''And who might have taught him that?'' As his mother, Claire was pretty sure she knew the answer to that question. ''Thanks to you two, I can do more plumbing than a lot of experts.''

''And who taught you everything you know?'' Ben puffed up his chest with mock pride.

''You, but some of it was by default. If you were

home from that hardware store more, I wouldn't have had to take apart as much plumbing.''

"True, but look at the education it's given you.''

That sounded like typical Ben. He always saw the bright side in things, at least where it was bound to benefit him. Claire made a face. ''That's one part of my education I could probably do without.''

"Yeah, Dad, how many times do you get asked to fix plumbing as a high-powered executive?'' Trent challenged.

"Never having been one, I can't tell you. However, I can point out that the people who fix plumbing for a living charge a pretty penny for doing so, and take their own sweet time. So if you know the basics, even as a high-powered executive, you'll be saving yourself time and money when the executive facilities need work.''

Claire shook her head. ''Not a problem I'm ever going to have to deal with. For The Caring Closet, the worst we'll have to handle is that leaky sink in the ladies' room at church. And I could actually fix that with a little patience and a couple of washers.''

She looked at her dinner crew. ''So, what's for dessert?''

Trent and Kyle both grinned. ''Brownies!'' they

chorused. "Are you surprised? Didn't think we could do that, did you, Mom," Kyle crowed.

"You're right. I'm impressed. If they're frosted and have nuts in them, I'll be just bowled over." Judging from the way they continued to grin, this was her lucky night.

Ben watched them head for the house. "They came out of a package. I didn't even know that you could do such a thing. You just unroll the brownie dough and put it in the pan, and bake it." He looked across the table at Claire. "That's not how you usually do it, I'm sure."

"True. But chocolate in any form is a plus right now. If I were doing the cooking, it wouldn't be much better, the way I'm tangled up in this project. You're doing a fine job, Ben." It was the truth, and she had to tell him so. After all, she had been quick to point out the mistakes he was making along the way. She still didn't want to think about the number of fleas that might be in the house.

Still, for the most part, life was good. Tiger lay on the grass chewing on a huge rawhide stick that was the size of a rolled-up newspaper. The boys were loping across the grass bringing a pan of brownies. Ben sat relaxed at the picnic table, the breeze ruffling his dark hair. This was more than just a growth experience. It was a gift from God. Claire intended to treasure it.

Kyle set down the brownies. "They have nuts, anyway. No icing, because we forgot to buy a can."

"No problem. If you do this again and want to fancy them up some even without icing, sprinkle powdered sugar on them after they cool down a little. So who's cutting me one? I'm surprised you haven't sampled them to see how they turned out."

"I thought about it," Trent confessed. "But your stuff never comes to the table with a corner missing, so I thought this shouldn't, either."

"That's only because she likes the middle best, and it's too obvious when it's gone."

Claire would have thumped Ben on the head, but he was absolutely right. This man knew her much too well.

It disturbed her that somewhere along the way she'd stopped knowing him as well. Maybe she was imagining it, but even in the midst of this wonderful evening, he looked troubled. She was pretty sure his expression had very little to do with Marcy. There was more to this whole problem than that—and Ben wasn't sharing.

Maybe he was going to make it, after all. Ben sat on the picnic bench, facing out toward the lawn, leaning up against the table. The pleasant summer evening kept everyone out on the grass long after they'd finished dinner. The boys and the dog were running up and down the yard playing keep-away with Tiger's big rawhide. He was a pretty game dog. Already he'd stolen it back twice from Kyle, and missed by inches when Trent had let his guard down for a moment.

Claire sat beside Ben, watching the action. Her ready laugh at the antics of boys and dog warmed his heart. A breeze played with strands of her cinnamon hair, and her eyes crinkled when she laughed. Even that didn't bring any wrinkles into the area around those marvelous eyes. How could that be? Ben knew he looked like a couple of miles of bad road, and he was only two years older than his wife. Yet, she still seemed no different from the girl he had married.

Maybe a little different, if he was honest, but he liked those differences. Maturity was a good thing; Claire had learned a great deal over the years.

His fingers ached to reach out and catch that stray hair, to tuck it in place, as she'd want it. But he wouldn't be able to stop there, he knew. Why did she have to move out to that apartment?

He knew the answer to that one. This was all his fault, with his stupid decision—from not telling her about the deal with Marcy to bringing home the moose-dog that was now running around the lawn. Even Claire, with her saint-like patience, could only take so much.

He had his family's best interest in mind, but it didn't seem to be getting him anywhere. He kept doing his best, working as hard as he knew how, taking on more responsibilities. And still, he felt like a failure.

Maybe that was what kept him from reaching out to her now, putting an arm around her and drawing her close. Claire seemed to have everything working out for her right now. Her project was on track, and it was something that was really going to help people. Best of all, she truly believed she was doing it all for God, and that He was pleased with her efforts.

If only he could remember a time when he'd felt that way. Sure, he was trying. Being a good father and husband wasn't easy, but he was holding up his end of that bargain. But running a hardware store for God? It didn't happen. Watching Trent run effortlessly, holding the dog's toy high above him while the beast leaped around his feet, Ben felt a different kind of ache.

He remembered what running had felt like when he was younger. The wind in your hair, running for the pure joy of it. That had seemed like something you could do and do it more for God than for anybody else. When had he lost some of the joy he felt every day? When he stopped playing football and real life took over—when he stopped being the golden boy?

It was so easy to wonder what life would be like now if he'd stuck with it. He sure wouldn't be worrying about a failing hardware store. Marcy wouldn't be in the picture, messing up his marriage in ways he couldn't understand. His boys would be much better provided for than they were now, and that dog would be some kind of pure breed they'd bought from a top kennel and paid good money for. Tiger wouldn't be a freebie from a grocery store parking lot.

And that would be better? A voice inside Ben's head nagged him. He pushed away the thought. Of course, life would be better if he'd stuck with his original game plan. That was the life he thought he had been meant to lead. Hadn't the college coach even said Ben had a chance at going pro if he stuck things out? Nobody had been more disappointed by Ben's decision to marry Claire than his football coach....

The bench shifted as Claire stood up, pulling Ben from his thoughts.

"You're leaving?" It seemed too soon for her to end the evening.

"I have to. There is a stack of paperwork still to be done, and I have to tag all the hangers. If we're really going to put this thing together in ten days, we all have to hustle." She ran her fingers through her hair. It made her look stressed.

Ben stood, anxious for a way to remove that stressed expression from her face. "Sure it can't wait just a little while? The lightning bugs will be coming out soon." He traced her cheek with one finger, enjoying the softness.

She made a noise in the back of her throat. "Tempting, very tempting." She moved her head to the side, planting a quick kiss on his fingers. "But with the lightning bugs come the mosquitoes. And those I could do without. See you in the morning."

She called goodbye to the boys, telling them she was going inside. "Can we go in too, Dad?"

"Before it gets dark?" He wondered if Trent was feeling okay.

"Yeah, for tonight. I got the book and I want to study for my permit test. I thought you could quiz me."

Ben felt a wave of shock run through him. "You're not actually old enough to take that thing?"

Trent's smile was broad. "Next Tuesday I am. You have to be exactly six months over fifteen to get your learner's permit now. And Tuesday's the day. I figured we could go down to the license office, and then maybe I could drive home.''

''If you pass,'' Ben pointed out.

Trent scoffed. ''Like I'd fail. It's only the written stuff for the permit. That reminds me, we need my birth certificate for proof. Do you know where it is?''

''Not exactly.'' Ben turned to ask Claire, but she had already crossed the grass to the apartment door and gone in, closing the door behind her. ''We'll ask your mother tomorrow.''

This little exchange had aged him about a decade. He was only thirty-five, and he had a son who would be old enough to drive a car next Tuesday.

A light went on in the living room of the apartment. Claire was going back to work, and he needed to, as well. ''Let's get this stuff cleaned up and then go in.'' He started picking up paper plates from the table. ''I guess we can study for that permit test.''

''Cool!''

Trent's voice rang with a joy Ben was sure he'd never feel again. How did things change so quickly? Or was it just life and reality, reminding him again that his precious dreams were only that? Dreams. Ben had never felt older than he did as he picked up condiment bottles from the table. And God and His joy had never seemed farther away.

The living room of this apartment was too quiet, and too empty. Claire was used to noise while she worked. She could probably turn on a ball game for atmosphere, but it wouldn't be the same without people making loud personal observations about the umpire's sight problems.

It still unnerved her a little that here, when she put down a pencil or her notebook full of lists, the items stayed exactly where she put them. There was no hunting for things that someone had borrowed. The paper didn't walk over to the phone where it was used for messages, and the pencil stayed right beside it on the coffee table. So this was what life was like if you were single, or at least had no children. It was odd.

Tagging the hangers had taken less time than she'd thought it would, and she had gone as far as she could go with things on her own. This left her time for something absolutely decadent, like a bubble bath no one would interrupt. It was a good thing she'd thought to pack bath salts to bring over here. She headed for the bathroom, which she knew would also be quiet, contain folded towels and even a scented mulberry candle.

She could definitely get used to this.

* * *

Ben and Trent were just about done studying for the permit test. At least, Ben was done. He could only take so much of this in one evening. Trent was picking up on some things rapidly. Others were going to be a problem no matter how many times they went over this stuff. He still got a little queasy at the thought of turning over his truck to a kid whose favorite game with toy cars used to be demolition derby.

The phone rang, and Kyle answered it in the kitchen. He was in the living room a few seconds later. "Dad, it's Mom. She sounds real funny and she wants to talk to you."

Ben got up and went into the kitchen. Why didn't Claire just come over if she needed something? His heart began to race. Maybe she'd hurt herself and couldn't move. Or maybe she just didn't want to see him again tonight. He picked up the phone. "Hey. What's up?" He tried to sound casual.

"Could you come over here? I need help." She sounded shaky.

"Sure. Should I bring any tools or anything?"

"No." There was a short pause. "Well, maybe some bug spray. Or a roll of paper towels or something."

There was a laugh building in him at gut level. He was going to have to work hard to suppress this one. "Spiders, huh?" It was the only thing that made Claire this shaky. She could handle bleeding kids, all manner of flying insects—even things that made *his* skin crawl, like legless reptiles. But spiders were a different story.

"Oh, Ben," she wailed. "It's one of those big fuzzy-looking ones that jump. And I was all ready to take a bath, and it's in the bathtub, and when I tried splashing it to drown it, it jumped instead, and it's still in the bathtub..." He could almost hear her shudder.

"Okay, calm down. I'll be over there in a minute. Is the door downstairs unlocked?"

"No. And I have the key that was in our kitchen."

"So you're going to need to come down the stairs and unlock the door. Providing that none of Mr. Spider's relatives are in the stairwell."

There was a smothered scream. "Oh, yuck. I hadn't even thought of that. And I'm barefoot. Oh, no. What if they are in there?"

If Claire had been getting ready for a bath, she was more than just barefoot. Ben tried to control his mirth as the picture of her inching down the stairwell in her altogether played in his mind. "Calm down. There aren't any other spiders, I'm sure. It's not like they travel in packs or anything. I'll be there in a minute, okay?"

"Okay." She still sounded emotional as she hung up the phone.

Ben whistled to himself. He got to rescue his wife from the big, bad spider. This he was going to enjoy.

Where was Ben? Surely he should be here by now. How long would it take to cross the yard? Claire stood in the living room, pacing in her short terry robe.

The ringing phone made her nearly jump out of her skin.

"Hello?"

"Hey. I'm going to be a bit, uh, detained."

"By what?"

There was silence on Ben's end of the phone. "Well, see, it's like this. I opened the back door to come out and kill the spider."

"Good. I'm glad you didn't walk through the screen." Claire was tight-lipped. What was the matter here?

"Yep. Opened that door, and there was a present for me on the nice, warm concrete porch. It even lifted up its head and said, 'Hi.'"

Claire's nervous tension evaporated. She had been so angry over the laughter she'd heard in Ben's voice—like he was some kind of hero killing the spider. Now she was fighting giggles. "Snake?"

She could hear him swallow, hard. "Good-size one, too."

Which meant it was anything more than a foot-long, pencil-width garden snake. "It's probably just that blue racer that lives under the hydrangea bushes." It would be fun to give him a hard time, for just a moment.

"We have a snake living in the yard? And you let it live there?" His voice held a note of panic.

"Well, sure. It eats bugs. It's perfectly harmless."

"I know. But it's a snake. And I am not going to step over it on the porch and give it the chance to bite me. I mean, what if you're wrong and it's a cottonmouth or something?"

"It's that blue racer. Sleeping on warm concrete. Why didn't you just ask one of the boys to move it?"

"Let's see, why didn't I do that?" He sounded irritated. "Maybe it's because I didn't want either of them to know how terrified the old man is of allegedly harmless reptiles. Or maybe it could be that once they pitch this sucker off the porch, he'll be in the grass, ticked off at whoever threw him off his nice warm spot. Take your pick."

"Oh. I see." The giggles were going to come out now; she couldn't help it. "I've got an idea. Let me put some shorts and a T-shirt on, and I'll come over there and get the washtub that the kids used to bathe the dog.''

She could hear the aggravation in his voice. ''Great. That will help a lot. Claire, even the tiniest snake will climb out of a washtub in nothing flat.''

There was no stopping the giggles. ''No, silly. I'm going to put it over him upside down. It won't thrill him any, but then you can walk around the washtub and come over here and kill the spider. Then when you go back to the house you can tell the guys we trapped a snake under the washtub for them to see. They can go let him loose—and everybody's happy.''

''Especially you, apparently. I hope you're enjoying this.''

''Immensely.'' It was the truth. And she'd almost forgotten her panic over the woolly spider in the bathtub.

''You know what I'm going to enjoy? My reward for getting rid of the spider. What should my payment be for killing him.''

Claire's skin shivered. She could feel his delight in her predicament. ''We'll talk about that one. I'll get dressed and trap the snake. Meet me on the porch.''

''I can hardly wait.'' He hung up the phone at his end, and Claire hurried to pull some clothes on. This was definitely going to be fun.

Chapter Twelve

Light from the streetlamp on the alley behind the garage played against the bedroom wall. Claire had never noticed it before. But then, she was noticing all kinds of things about this room that she'd never noticed before. It was funny that the bed, which had seemed so vast and uncomfortable for one, wasn't all that spacious for two. Yet she knew that if she rolled over right now and settled in, she'd have the best night's sleep she'd gotten in a week. After sixteen years of marriage, she liked being a little crowded, as long as Ben was doing the crowding.

Still, she couldn't just roll over and go to sleep holding onto Ben as if he were a teddy bear. This surprising interlude hadn't settled anything between them. And, to be practical, they were out in the apartment, and it was still very early. The kids would wonder soon what was going on. It was probably time to nudge her valiant rescuer out of his doze and send him back to the enemy camp.

It was harder and harder to think of the house that way. She'd asked for guidance from the Lord over this situation, and if the last few hours weren't proof enough for her, she wasn't sure what would be. They'd already gone through fleas, snakes and spiders. That was close enough to the plagues of Eqypt for her to relent.

She still couldn't just do so, however, without some answers from her husband. "Okay, my friend, up and at 'em," she murmured in Ben's ear. "The snake awaits, remember?"

"How could I forget?"

He didn't sound totally awake. As he rolled over, she could see the slow, easy smile on his face. Even in the low light from the street lamp, his eyes shone and those even, white teeth were visible.

"Watching you trap that critter was something else. Especially wearing jeans and a bathrobe. What a combination. But whatever possessed you to go barefoot? Weren't you afraid he'd bite you?"

Claire sighed. At least, it started out a sigh. It ended up a soft, almost feline yawn of contentment. "I told you before, he's just a bug eater from the garden. Not harmful or unfriendly. Although I can't promise he'll be thrilled to have spent this much time under a washtub."

"Hey, I'll warn the boys before I let them out to look at the snake." He shivered next to her— not from cold, Claire knew, because the room was plenty warm. It was just saying the word *snake* that made her big, tough husband shudder. Of course if she were to talk about the woolly jumping thing he had dispatched in the bathroom, she'd shudder—so they were even.

"I think I'm almost ready for a truce. I know that makes me the loser in our battle of wills, but I miss you too much." Claire sat up as she spoke, unwilling to admit her weakness while Ben could see her face. "I still need some answers, though."

He was up after her, an arm around her shoulders. "You know there are some I can't give you."

Claire could feel her muscles tighten. "I know there's some you *think* you can't give me. Why didn't you tell me that your big secret business meeting last week was a trip to the ball game?"

Now his grip on her tightened. "What difference does that make?"

"When someone sees you there and starts drawing conclusions, and coming to me for answers, plenty." All the comfort she'd felt with Ben was beginning to evaporate.

"That's ridiculous."

"I know it is. And I didn't say I believed anything odd was happening. But this whole secret business seems to be getting out of hand."

When Ben didn't answer, Claire went on, mostly to fill the uncomfortable silence. "I'm willing to agree to your partial truce, Ben. God's been steering me in that direction, anyway. I already prayed with Gloria about it all and asked Him to show me His way in all this."

"And you think all the spiders and snakes and such are a sign from God?" Ben didn't sound all that convinced.

"I actually do. Don't you see things that way?" Claire felt irritation creeping in at Ben's skepticism.

"Honestly? No. I've asked God for a nice, clear sign on something more than once in my life, and I've never exactly gotten a message written in lights. What makes you so very special?"

She backed up, surprised by the ferocity of his statement. "Nothing. No one of us is more special in God's eyes, Ben. You know that as well as I do."

"Do I? I'm not sure I know much at all about God's eyes right now. Or the rest of Him. We haven't exactly been best buds lately." Even in the low light she could see the glimmer of pain in his eyes. "I'm struggling here, Claire. I have no idea what God wants me to do anymore, or if He'd tell me even if I flat-out asked. Don't get me wrong. I know He's still up there someplace. But as far as caring about my daily life, I don't know if He really does. And it's been quite some time since I've been sure of anything like that."

He finished fastening his khakis and bent down for the T-shirt someplace on the floor. Finding it, he pulled it over his head in a fluid motion that she would have admired under other circumstances. Right now, she was too stunned by his admission.

This was more surprising than his earlier comment that, given the chance, he might live life over in a different way. And it gave Claire the same cold, hollow feeling inside. As if she'd lost her anchor. This bothered her more than anything he could have said about Marcy.

"How could this be? And when were you going to tell me about it?"

"I just did, didn't I?" His voice was rough.

"I guess so. But Ben, how long has this been? And what can we do about it?"

"*We* can't do anything about it. I'd say this is strictly a problem between God and me. And He's not taking my calls right now. The line seems to be busy.''

Her head was spinning. Claire got up off the bed and went around to where Ben stood. His head was down and he was interested in slipping into his shoes without losing his balance. ''That's just not right. That's nothing like the way I know God works in our lives. And it's nothing like what I'd expect from you, either.''

''Well, get used to it, because it's the way I feel right now. You keep asking for honesty and sharing. Well, I'm sharing the feelings that bother me the most right now. I feel like that God you talk about who's so wonderful and your best friend is about a million miles away.'' He shrugged off her embrace and headed toward the doorway.

Claire's arms felt empty. ''Yeah, well if He feels that far away, who moved?'' She sank back down on the bed. She was too stunned to cry, even when Ben's footsteps faded and the door to the apartment slammed on the first floor. It was nearly half an hour before she could force herself up to check to see if he'd locked up behind himself. He had.

Claire shook her head. Even in the depths of a problem like this one, Ben had kept taking care of his family. He just couldn't let go of any of the burden, hand anything over to anybody else, even God. No wonder God seemed so far away for him.

Going back upstairs to the darkened apartment was what finally brought on her tears.

Ben was staring at the ceiling again, hours after everybody else had settled down. Why did he feel so bad? He'd had a wonderful, unexpected interlude with his wife, followed by getting something off his chest that had lingered for way too long. Shouldn't he feel great? Instead, he just felt numb. Would he ever get rid of this deadened feeling?

Claire's words kept echoing in his ears. She was right; he had to admit that. If God felt far away, it was because *Ben* had moved. Wasn't this how a man was supposed to be, though? It was the example he'd always seen from his father, from Claire's dad, from most men he knew. You shouldered your own burdens, dealt with your own problems. You didn't expect anybody else to do it for you. Not even God. But that tough guy stance just wasn't working for him anymore. He felt incredibly tired and incredibly alone.

The dog was whining again. Now he actually had an excuse for not sleeping. He let the noise go on a few minutes, then swung his feet over the side of the bed. Padding downstairs in ratty gym shorts, he looked for Kyle in the dog's nest in the pantry. For a change the boy wasn't there with Tiger.

Maybe even the kid got tired of sleeping with the dog once in a while.

"Come on, then. You and I will go out in the backyard and look at the stars," he told the beast. The dog's huge brindle tail beat a rhythm of agreement on the floor, while Ben got the leash.

Outside, the night was starry, and Ben could enjoy all the glimmering points of light. The dog snuffled happily in the grass, looking for rabbit trails. "That is not what we're out here for," Ben reminded him. Tiger paid attention for only a moment before another animal scent got him all distracted and Ben had to tug on the leash. It was a good thing he'd stopped to fasten it on this mutt. Without it, he'd be halfway across Friedens in the dark by now.

Looking down at the fractious dog, Ben mused. Maybe that was his own problem right now. Maybe he'd just slipped the lead God had intended for him and was running in the dark, alone. God provided so many ways to keep His children close: Scripture reading, prayer, a dozen different groups at church Ben could be a part of if he chose. Maybe it was time to find that welcome tether for himself.

Those endless locker-room talks from high school and college tugged at his mind the way Tiger tugged on the leash. How many times had he heard a coach tell him to fake it until he made it? If you acted as if something were already true, it became true in time. He'd been waiting for some huge divine inspiration to come and hit him, welcome him back into the fold.

That wasn't how things worked with God, if Ben remembered right. That divine "hit" had come some two thousand years ago in Bethlehem and Jerusalem through Jesus. He shouldn't need another reminder.

He was still staring up at the stars, thinking and wondering. Apparently he'd been there a while, because Tiger had stopped pulling on the leash and had now doubled back to nuzzle at his hand. The dog plopped down in the grass next to Ben. Tongue lolling out of his puppy face, he seemed to be asking when they were going back inside.

"All right. Let's move."

The tail thumped on the grass, and Tiger sprang up to join him.

Funny that it took spiders, snakes and a whining dog to start him back on the path the way God intended. It was an unlikely combination. But what he knew about God boiled down to very few things, and one of them was definitely that all things were possible for Him, and he used everything to His purpose. Maybe, just maybe, it was time that He started using Ben again.

Ben's jog back to the house with Tiger felt more like prayer than anything had in a long time.

In the morning Ben woke up to the smell of coffee brewing. It had to be an hallucination, because there was definitely the scent of bacon, as well. As much as he loved his kids, he knew their limitations, and cold cereal was the one and only breakfast they could make.

Still, as he showered and dressed, there was still that enticing smell coming up the stairs. Could Claire have come back home? He felt like a kid at Christmas, trying not to take the stairs three at a time on his way down.

She looked more beautiful than usual—and not just because she was at the stove flipping pancakes. This was definitely his Claire back, standing in the kitchen barefoot in old denim shorts and a T-shirt left over from one of the boys' sports camps. In Ben's eyes she had never looked lovelier.

"Hey." It wasn't the cleverest of greetings. But if he tried anything profound, Ben thought, he might choke up.

Claire turned from the stove. Her smile was sweetness itself. "I lay awake most of the night thinking I ought to be over here. Regretting what I said to you. This is not giving in, though. It's just breakfast."

"I'll take it. Cold cereal has gotten kind of old."
He walked into her arms and savored the feel of
the cloud of her soft hair as her head tucked into
his chest. This was home. This was right. "And
don't feel like you have to apologize for anything.
You were right."

"Right or not, I wasn't kind or sympathetic.
What I said and the way I said it was probably the
last thing you needed to hear."

"It was, actually. After hearing that, things
seemed to fall into place." He nuzzled the top of
her head, thinking she had never felt better in his
arms. And already regretting that he either had to
let her go, or eat a burnt breakfast. Hungry as he
was for her touch, he was even hungrier for pancakes and bacon. So Ben let go of his wife, kissed
her forehead and pointed her back to the stove.

"Can I at least pour us coffee?" He went for
mugs in the cabinet.

"Sure. It's neat, watching you work your way
around the kitchen. You caught on, didn't you."

"Like I had a choice? It was catch on or starve.
And your sons aren't very forgiving."

"*My* sons? I didn't teach them to eat like that,
for sure. Or that wrestling stuff they do all the time.
They're not just mine."

"No, they aren't. And I'm surprised they're not
down here already wolfing down breakfast."

"They've been and gone. I fixed a batch of pancakes and bacon for them while you showered, and they're out at the picnic table. Probably giving the dog pancake bits and bacon crumbs with syrup." Claire grimaced. "That beast is going to be spoiled rotten."

"Probably. But it does mean we get to eat breakfast alone."

She set a plate of pancakes in front of him at the table. "True. He might be worth every penny you paid for him." Ben was on his second strip of bacon before he remembered that Claire knew the dog was free.

He lazed over breakfast as long as he could. Claire seemed in no hurry to move, either. He was surprised, given the amount of work that he imagined awaited her in the apartment. "Will you be back for dinner?" he asked. Maybe not the most romantic thing he could find out, but pretty critical to his plans for the evening.

"Only if you're cooking. Like I said, this wasn't admitting defeat. It was just breakfast."

"And a pleasant one. Of course I'm cooking. About the only thing left that I can do is chili, or steaks on the grill. It's too hot to cook chili inside, so it will have to be steaks."

"Great. I'll see that the guys make a salad, and maybe when you pick up the steaks you can get a loaf of French bread to go with them. We don't need much more.''

He picked up her hand and brought it to his lips. "I don't need anything more, myself. I've got what I need for now. Thanks, babe." He hadn't meant to make her cry; he hated to see her cry. Maybe that was why he didn't say anything even vaguely mushy most of the time. It always brought on the waterworks.

"Oh, Ben. I don't mean to upset you, really." She was apologizing for her tears. Didn't she know that was the one thing that bothered him more than her crying? "You're so sweet, sometimes it's hard to believe. A tough guy with a heart of gold."

That was more than he deserved. It made him uncomfortable to listen to her compliments. Especially when he knew how little he did to earn them. When he added that to the fact that he was late for work, and the kids would be bursting in any minute, he had plenty of reasons to get up.

"You wish," he said, trying to sound tough. It didn't work. Claire knew him in ways he didn't know himself. And he loved every minute of it.

He hustled out to work. Maybe he was a couple of minutes late getting there, but today it didn't seem to matter as much. He was still there long before opening, and even if he hadn't been, Pete could have opened the store.

Ben was deeply involved with inventory and stock records, when Marcy breezed into his office unannounced. At first he thought he'd lost track of time. They weren't supposed to be meeting until one, and it couldn't be that late yet. He looked up at the clock, relieved to find it was only twelve-fifteen.

"I misjudged how long it would take me to get here in the middle of the day." Not only was Marcy overdressed, as usual, but she was a bad liar. Ben knew that most of her family still lived here in town, and Marcy had to know how long it took to get from St. Louis to Friedens in any type of weather, any time of day. Would he have to start pointing out some of these little inconsistencies? Maybe when they got to negotiations. At this point, they were both dancing around bona fide offers for his company, and he had to be nice.

"Anyway, I haven't had lunch yet. Is that place out on the highway that they're now calling Ethyl's Diner any good?"

"Passable. Not as good as the Milk Shake Barn," Ben said, referring to the original restaurant on the site. "Want to try it, anyway?"

Marcy shrugged in a way that was probably intended to be artful and look unrehearsed. "Sure. It might be fun."

"I'll drive. If you don't mind a truck."

Her nose wrinkled a little, but she still agreed. Ben looked at her outfit again. Clearly, she hadn't anticipated riding in anything with mud flaps. Didn't this woman own any clothing without a short, slim skirt? He didn't see how she ever got an honest day's work done in these getups.

Ethyl's Diner was supposed to look like the real thing, circa 1968. Ben could have told them that they didn't get it quite right. Not that he had vivid memories back that far, but the whole place had a plastic, fake feel about it. He ordered a burger and onion rings, watching as Marcy got herself a diet soda and a salad. Guess she had to keep fitting into those skinny skirts.

"So, I hear things aren't what they used to be around your house."

Her comment caught him with a glass of ice water halfway to his lips. He didn't spill it. And he didn't gape at her. Ben gave himself points for composure. "Oh? And just what did you hear?"

"I've been talking to my cousin Linda. And she says Claire's moved out of the house." Marcy batted her eyelashes. "I'd really hate to think our business deal has been the cause of friction between you. If there's anything I can do…"

Ben felt his face stiffen. "Well, your cousin's wrong. So, no, there's nothing you can do." That came out more like a bark than he might have wanted. But he couldn't help it.

"All right. But remember, I'm here for you if you need a sympathetic shoulder. I've been through the whole divorce thing, and I know it's no picnic."

Ben didn't respond. Hadn't the woman heard him? The answer to that question was instantly clear when he realized that Marcy's warm hand was patting his arm. Part of that sympathy thing she was talking about, he guessed. Ben felt like slamming his water glass down on the table. How could he have been so dense?

This wasn't just business for her. Claire had been right on that score all along. And now he was stuck in negotiations he was unsure of, with a woman who had her own personal agenda. This was going to be some lunch. He eased his arm out from under her grasp as gently as possible. Suddenly he had no appetite whatsoever.

Chapter Thirteen

The phone rang while Claire was straightening her blouse. She picked up the receiver, hoping it wasn't anyone with a problem for the grand opening of The Caring Closet today.

"So, how many times have you changed clothes this morning?" Ben asked teasingly.

"None. I have a designated outfit, remember? And don't say good morning or anything." Claire stuck out her tongue at the phone, as if he were in the room with her.

"Sorry. I've been up and out for so long, it didn't dawn on me that it was still morning."

"Awww." She tried to put real sympathy into the expression. "Did you see Mr. Snake this morning?"

"Nope. Maybe he was a sign or something. I mean, since you moved back into the house, he hasn't shown up. And you haven't needed me for any more spider killing."

Claire could hear the grin in his voice. She shivered, thinking of those spiders.

"So, what *are* you wearing?"

"That navy suit I showed you yesterday, remember? I think it was probably Gloria's." Claire smoothed down the skirt. For once, she had to give the Grady-Trump sisters credit for a marvelous idea. Peggy had contacted all the media for the grand opening; Patsy had come up with the "hook," that special idea that meant someone might actually have enough interest to come.

It was very simple: the committee members who had worked the most on getting the facility ready would each go through the coordination process, just as would a client getting set up for a job interview. Then they'd wear the outfit, picked out with them in mind, to the grand opening. Patsy had beamed at the approval she'd gotten over her idea. And Claire had enjoyed every moment of the group's work to dress the Grady-Trump "girls," as they called themselves, along with Gloria and herself.

The only stipulation that Claire made was that no one could wear anything they'd donated to the project. Which is how she found herself wearing a very flattering navy suit this morning and resisting the urge to straighten the blouse again.

"I've got to go in a few minutes."

"This early? Nobody will be there yet."

"That's the point. I'll see you there in a while, okay?"

"Definitely. Good luck."

"Thanks." Claire hung up the phone and looked at the receiver. Maybe this had been a growth experience for Ben, after all. He did quite a bit around the house these days. Things had gone much smoother once she'd moved back in to sleep at home, at least.

Her daytime hours in the last ten days had still been spent in the apartment. She treated it the way she would any other job: getting up from the breakfast table, dressing and tidying up after herself, then leaving. But before dinnertime every night, she came home.

If anybody had asked her several weeks ago whether her husband and sons were capable of learning to take care of themselves, she would have told them no. Nothing on earth, she'd have said, would get the three Jericho men to learn to do laundry, cook and pick up after themselves. But they had. And they didn't even complain about it anymore.

Even Tiger was beginning to fit in. It would be months before he matured into a well-trained house dog. Right now, he was still all puppy, and most of the puppy seemed to be feet and tail. He knocked over almost anything he explored, but he did so with such innocent delight that it was hard to be upset with him.

Tiger had graduated to having the run of the place, as long as there was someone in the house with him. Accidents got fewer and farther between with each week. In fact, Claire couldn't remember being consulted on puppy cleanup all last week. Of course, that could have been because lately she was only at the apartment about a third of the time. She'd made endless trips to church, delivering clothing and racks. Ben had cheerfully swapped vehicles with her for several days so she could use the truck for hauling most of The Caring Closet donations.

Between Ben's truck and the minivan motorcade of the rest of the volunteers, things had gotten transferred with few problems. Now all that was left was for Claire to fret over the grand opening of The Caring Closet facilities. The congregation had toured as part of Sunday night activities at the chapel last night, and Claire had to admit that everything had gone very well.

This morning was the big event, and she was

much more nervous than she'd been last night. Today they would welcome people such as the mayor and county newspaper reporters. There might even be somebody from one of the St. Louis television stations, if it was a slow news day in the city. Claire resisted an urge to straighten her blouse again, and went to the closet to get her suit jacket.

She breathed a quick prayer while she put on the last touches of makeup and slid into her dressy sandals. As she fastened the straps, she called down the stairs to the boys so they'd put Tiger in his pantry hideaway before she came down the stairs. No sense sacrificing a perfectly good pair of panty hose to the hound.

It took both boys to get Tiger corralled. Trent was rearranging his hair by the time Claire got to the kitchen. He looked neat but a little winded.

"Surely, dealing with one little puppy can't be that hard a task for the junior varsity quarterback," she teased, looking for her purse.

"I think this dog is going to get me in shape for two-a-days," Trent said. "He gives me as much fight as anybody on the field so far."

"At least, he didn't slobber up my shirt."

Kyle appreciated clean laundry more now that he had a hand in producing it. Claire wondered why she hadn't turned over some of these responsibilities a long time ago.

Claire picked up her car keys. "Ready to go?"

Kyle nodded. "Are we meeting Dad there?"

"He'll be there eventually. I don't expect him as early as we'll get there," Claire told her youngest son. Ben had promised to be there before the grand opening ceremonies began. She knew he had plenty to do at the store, so Claire was particularly grateful for his support. She still wasn't sure how much he approved of the whole idea. He'd been more encouraging in the last ten days—or at least less argumentative. Of course, she suspected that had something to do with the fact that the store and house, and whatever business deal he had cooking with Marcy, had him much busier than usual. With so little time for them to spend together, she suspected, he just didn't have the energy to argue.

It suited her better to spend it as they had, anyway. They both slept better in that big bed upstairs together. Ben tossed and turned in it some, still, and he wasn't sharing all his problems. But he had admitted to working through his faith difficulties, and Claire saw his Bible open and splayed on the nightstand more evenings than not. She yearned to try and heal his wounds, whatever they were. Still, that firm wall Ben built around himself remained in place most of the time. It was rare for him to let a brick slip.

She breathed a prayer just for him, and hustled the kids into the car to head for church. If she weren't so dressed up, she would have suggested walking the three short blocks. That wouldn't do however, on a hot August day when she wanted to look her best.

There were already a fair number of cars in the Friedens Chapel parking lot when they got there. Linda was getting out of her minivan, shooing her kids into the building, as the Jerichos got out of the truck. Claire scanned the lot for her own car, but it wasn't there yet. Not that she expected Ben to leave Pete in charge for that long, but she could always hope.

Fifteen minutes later, the mayor was there, and the pastor was ready to start the ceremonies. Claire was still holding off, waiting for more people. It didn't surprise her much that Ben still hadn't arrived, but it was odd that Gloria and Hank hadn't put in an appearance. Gloria was early for everything, and Hank was almost as punctual as his bride. There was a definite lack of family here, and Claire was getting nervous.

Trent and Kyle were off to one side, chatting with other youth group kids. She knew that if things were delayed much longer, the boys would take the cover off the foosball table in the youth room next door, and wouldn't be seen for an hour or more. If it weren't for the noise the game made, she'd encourage it just to give them something to do. However, four or five teenagers playing a noisy game could easily drown out the grand opening speeches. Better to leave them talking among themselves but still behaving.

Five minutes later, Claire was out of stalling techniques and out of patience. Her whole family, other than the ones she'd brought herself, appeared to have better things to do. Even Carrie wasn't among the crowd filling the fellowship hall. *They better have a very good reason for this.* Claire counted to ten, then gave up. It wasn't going to calm her down this morning. She caught the pastor's eye over the line of people separating them and motioned for him to go ahead with his opening remarks and prayer.

She used the time herself to try to turn her thoughts to the work at hand. There was no sense mentally berating Ben or the rest of her family. Their failure to show up this morning didn't lessen this accomplishment. Peggy and Patsy were here, smiling with pleasure as they were introduced.

Linda's brood started a "wave" when their mom was recognized as part of the steering committee, and she turned bright pink. Trent's expression told her she had nothing to worry about on that score. And a few minutes later, there was a lot of youth group cheering when the pastor got her up to the podium to speak.

Claire wasn't sure afterward exactly what she'd said. Without having Ben to focus on, as she normally would during a dreaded public speaking opportunity, she lost her train of thought a bit. Kyle provided her with an image much like his father to look at, but he was even worse than Ben would have been, waggling his eyebrows and smiling at her during the serious moments.

She got through her note cards without major disaster, then helped lead the crowd into the side room where The Caring Closet would do most of the work of the project. While flashes popped and video cameras whirred, the mayor and Nessa cut the ribbon strung across the door. Everyone cheered.

After a short tour, made even shorter by the size of the crowd compared to the smallish room, everyone went back to Fellowship Hall. Claire looked out over the crowd again, still wondering about her absent family. Probably at least three good excuses there. Or, at least, one good excuse from Hank and Gloria. Carrie could be on an emergency call, which would even explain her father's absence if anything really big had happened. She didn't want to think that Ben had just gotten involved with something at the store and lost track of time. Surely only a crisis would have kept him away.

The fashion show was over and Claire was still wearing her pasted-on smile, when Ben walked into the room. She broke off a conversation with one of the newspaper reporters, apologizing, to talk to her errant husband. The moment she saw him, the words of complaint she had ready died on her lips.

There was no sparkle in his blue eyes. His shoulders were set as if ready for a tackle. Brows knit to a nearly straight line, he'd picked up a boy with each hand by the time he'd crossed the room to Claire.

"What's the matter?" Claire blurted. There wasn't any question in her mind that something was wrong. Please, let it be something they could deal with, something they could fix.

"Carrie called me at the store. She was at your dad's. Gloria's trying to talk him into going to the hospital and she wanted reinforcements."

"The hospital?" Claire felt her knees getting shaky. "What for?"

"He didn't feel good. Of course, he said he'd just had a physical and it wasn't anything more than heartburn from too much coffee at breakfast. But Gloria wasn't buying that and neither was your sister."

"Where is he?" Claire tried to remember where her purse was and if her keys were in it. Maybe this would be a good time for Trent to practice his driving skills; she was sure that at the moment they would be better than hers.

"I went over there and agreed with Gloria and Carrie that he looked awful," Ben said. "So he agreed to go to the hospital and let me come get you here. He didn't like that last part—said he was sure this was a lot of nonsense over nothing and we were dragging you away from your big day. But I knew you'd never forgive yourself, or me, if things turned out bad."

His arms were around her then, giving Claire the shelter and support she needed. Her head was swimming with shock. Was this really a heart attack? Ben and Carrie obviously thought so. They wouldn't have urged her father to the hospital unless they were worried. Where had she left her things? She didn't have time to wonder.

There was a hand on her shoulder. "I couldn't help overhearing." Peggy handed Claire her purse. "Patsy and I will make sure the reception goes on and somebody talks to all the reporters. Nessa's here, and she can do anything we forget about. Go on now. You have to get going."

Claire wiped a stray tear off her cheek. It was surprising to see Peggy this confident, and her sister Patsy only half a step behind her and in full agreement for a change. "Yes, go on, please," Patsy added. "We can handle this. It certainly isn't any more challenging than Saturday detention used to be."

The mental picture added a note of levity to an otherwise grim situation. "Thank you both, so much."

Claire let Ben lead her out of the hall into the hot sunshine. Behind them the boys were silent, exchanging glances.

Nothing this serious had ever happened to them that they were old enough to remember. Trent had still been a toddler when her mother died, Kyle not even born yet. Claire prayed all the way to the doors of the emergency room. Even so, she was nervous. Why couldn't Carrie have lent them her car with the siren and flashing lights so they could get there faster?

When they got to the emergency room, Claire hugged her sister, hard. Carrie hugged back, but it wasn't the strong hug that she expected. Her younger sister felt like a little girl in her arms instead of the boisterous woman she usually was. Her face was so pale that her tan freckles stood out in relief across the bridge of her nose.

"You're a funny color," Claire told her.

"Not as funny as Daddy. You wouldn't believe

what it took to get him in here. Claire, I was so scared. Thank heavens for your husband.''

"I've said that before. Although, not in a hospital emergency room." She turned to Ben, who had followed her in after parking the car. "What did you tell him that made him listen when nobody else could get him to?"

Ben shrugged. "I only pointed out that he was upsetting his wife and his daughter. That it wouldn't hurt to check things out and prove them wrong, but if he proved them right by keeling over on the way to your reception, we were all going to be real ticked off."

Claire had to smile. She was pretty sure Ben had edited those remarks for present company. "Blunt, but it worked. Has Gloria come out here lately?"

Carrie shook her head. "No, and they won't let me stay with them all the time. Something about my knowing too much about their stupid monitors. I'm still scared. What if he arrests and they don't catch things in time?"

Claire hadn't ever seen her sister this shaken. With all her training, she usually handled every emergency like the pro that she was. Of course, most emergencies weren't happening to her own father. "He's in the right place, and you helped him get here. We have to leave the rest in God's hands. Want to start praying here or in there?"

"In there first." Carrie took her arm. "You have to see him to understand what we're talking about."

She wanted to tell Carrie that she wasn't so sure she wanted to see Daddy right now. That it was scary enough that he was ill. Seeing it might make her lose the little composure she had left. Still, she allowed Carrie to take her back to the curtained area, where she could hear Hank and Gloria talking softly.

When she parted the curtains and walked in, her knees felt wobbly. Her father was an odd dusky shade, and he was sweating as if he were outside on this hot day, not in a chilly emergency room. Even with no medical training, Claire knew this was not a good sign. Gloria perched on a chair, as close to the gurney as she could get. She looked as if she could launch herself from her seat in about half a second. Claire knew she would, too, if she thought Hank needed anything.

"Sorry about this, Claire." Her father's voice sounded rough, strained. "They insisted I come in here. I told them I'd go after your opening, but that husband of yours is a stubborn guy."

"Almost as stubborn as the woman you married," Gloria told him, looking tense. "There is no way any of us were letting you go anyplace but here."

Hank sighed. "I know. And I have to admit, you're probably right. But I don't have time for all this right now." He looked at Claire. "Don't go calling your sister yet and scaring her. Wait until we find out if they're keeping me here awhile or not."

"I will," Claire told him. It was mainly to reassure her father. She was already sure that she'd be calling Laurel, and that the doctors would be keeping her father. But if he wanted a little bit of control in this situation, she was willing to let him have it. That scrap of control might be the only thing they could hang onto, for a few hours, at least. That, and the prayers she knew Gloria was already saying silently as she sat with her hand on Hank's shoulder. "And I'll be out there waiting and praying, Dad."

His look grew more solemn, but less pained. "Do that. No matter what's going on, I could use the prayers. I'm a little distracted myself right now."

That admission made Claire as scared as she knew Carrie was. For Hank Collins to be worried about himself, he had to feel terribly sick.

Chapter Fourteen

By noon, they'd been in the emergency room for more than an hour. Ben let go of Claire's hand and started pulling out his wallet. He reached in and handed her all the bills that he fished out. She looked at the money, than handed him back a ten-dollar bill. "Get the guys lunch on the way home. This still leaves me with plenty for whatever comes up."

"Okay. But let me give you quarters, too." Ben stood, reaching into his pockets. "I wish I had a cell phone."

"So when this is over, we'll get one." Claire told him. She took the change he handed her, wondering what she was going to do with the fistful of quarters until she needed them. This was where men's clothing was much more practical. Her slim navy suit didn't have the kind of pockets for change that every man took for granted. Even in her purse, that many quarters were going to be heavy and awkward.

Ben leaned over and kissed her forehead. "Call me the minute you hear anything. I'll be at home." His blue eyes were bright with concern.

"I will. Promise me you'll pray for us," Claire said as she hugged him. He didn't respond, but even his curt nod was comforting. She knew Ben still struggled with whatever demons had been haunting him lately, but that somehow the way would get easier.

By three in the afternoon, Claire was ready to tell whoever picked out her interview sandals that they needed a shorter heel. Her feet were cramped, with knots in the arches. She'd paced the corridors near the emergency room, and made several runs for cold drinks or coffee for Carrie and Gloria.

She'd checked home with Ben twice, keeping him updated on her father's progress. Hank was stable, and the fact that he'd had a "minor" heart attack, according to the doctor on duty, had been confirmed. Soon he would be transferred to the cardiac care unit upstairs.

"I'll feel better once he's moved up there," Gloria confided in Claire and Carrie on one of their rare trips out to the hall together. "I know the staff are good. Mike's told me Friedens has an excellent emergency room. But I'll feel better when everybody taking care of him is someone who has knowledge of heart problems."

Carrie leaned her head on Gloria's shoulder. "Mike's right about the emergency department here. But I'm with you. I'll feel better when he's upstairs." She straightened and looked at Claire. "You think it's time to call Laurel?"

"Probably. I still don't know how much to tell her."

"Tell her everything we know for sure," Gloria said. "Don't keep her in the dark trying to spare her feelings."

"And tell her that we're not likely to stay here in the long run."

Carrie's comment surprised Claire. She hadn't thought past the move upstairs, but her sister knew more about the medical aspects of her dad's condition.

"What do you think will happen next?"

Carrie took a deep breath and closed her eyes for a minute. They were clear when she opened them again, but she still sounded shaky. "The way the ER doc described things, I'm willing to bet Dad'll be a bypass surgery candidate in the next couple days. And if that's the case, it won't happen here. We'll be at Washington General.''

When Claire thought about that, it made sense. The bigger town another ten miles past Union had a much larger hospital. Doctors on staff there were experienced, usually affiliated with St. Louis medical schools and teaching hospitals, as well.

"This is serious stuff. I better call Laurel now, just so I don't shock her with too much news at once.''

Carrie wrinkled her brow. "You know she's going to get all upset no matter what. She was just out here less than six weeks ago for the wedding, and now she's going to want to come back.''

"I know. What do we tell her?''

"To hold off on that.'' Gloria squared her shoulders. "She has a son and a house to take care of in California. No sense flying out here yet. If it's necessary, then we'll let her. Go call. I'm going in with your dad again.''

Claire mentally called up her sister's phone number. It took a moment. Usually she could dial Laurel in her sleep, but her brain was fuzzy right now. Laurel would know something was wrong the moment she heard who was on the phone. Claire never called during the middle of the day when the rates were so high. *Lord, hold me up through this,* she prayed. Telling her sister fifteen hundred miles away about the current situation was harder than facing her father in pain.

By four, the calls had been made, Hank was in a room in the cardiac care unit, and Claire was impressed by Carrie's call on the situation. Hank's new cardiologist sat in the room with all of them, explaining why he'd only be Hank's doctor for a few hours.

"Once we're sure you're stable enough for an ambulance ride, you'll be going to General. The tests we need to run can be done there more easily. There's a good chance you could be facing surgery in the next couple of days, and General would be my choice if I were having that kind of work done."

"I understand." Hank's color was a little better, and he was sitting up in bed. He was connected with more tubes than Claire liked to see, but she knew they were all necessary. "Do we have to go the ambulance route, though? My daughter here is a Fire & Rescue officer, and my wife's son is a lead EMT. Can't we just—"

"Oh, no." Carrie's voice was firm. "You are not leaving this place in my car. Or Mike's truck. I know the thought of an ambulance ride over to General doesn't thrill you, Dad, but I'm not taking that kind of responsibility."

"She's right, Hank." Gloria put a hand on his

arm. "You'd never forgive yourself if something went wrong. Let's do it their way, even if you don't like the sound of it."

Hank shrugged. "Fine. I guess I'm just used to calling my own shots."

"And as Sheriff, that's a great thing," the doctor said. "But as a cardiology patient, you have to surrender a lot of control. I know that isn't easy, and I appreciate your effort. I'll come by at General in a couple days to see how things go. Good luck to you." He shook Hank's hand and left the room.

Claire didn't know what to make of her father's expression as he watched the doctor leave.

"Well, that's five in my collection now," he said with a look of consternation.

"Collection of what, Dad?"

"Good luck wishes." He turned to Carrie. "You all do that, you know. When you leave a patient, you don't say goodbye. Everybody from the technicians in X-ray to the ER people to the guy who moved my bed up here says the same thing. 'Good luck to you,' they say. Do I really need that much good luck right now?"

"A little more can never hurt, Dad." Carrie's voice was soft. "But I'd rather rely on prayer. It makes me feel better."

"Me too, kiddo." Her father took her hand. He

looked over at Claire. "Think it's about time to call somebody over at the Chapel so they can come by and pray over me before they move me? We're going to keep the ministry staff hopping, I think."

Her father was back in control of the situation, as much as he could be. Somehow, that lifted Claire's spirits as she went to make her calls.

Ben stood in the doorway of Hank's new room at Washington General, watching Claire and the rest of the women get him settled in. This had been an incredibly long day, and he was sure that for Gloria, Carrie and Claire, it felt endless.

He tried to sound stern when he spoke. "I mean it, now. I want at least two of you to take the car that I left in the lot and go home. Shower, change clothes, eat something. Even sleep if you can. I'm kicking you all out for a while. Maybe even until morning."

"I'll take you up on the offer. But not the car. Mine is already here, and I can drive it easier. I'd have to look for the controls in yours, and I'm too tired to do that. I'd be washing the windshield when I wanted to signal a left turn," Carrie said.

She and Claire both looked pale and exhausted.

Gloria put a hand on Hank's shoulder. "I'm going to take him up on his offer for a little while. Carrie can take me home, and after I spend a little while there, Mike will bring me back for a while tonight.'' She looked up at Ben. ''This does mean you're offering to stay, right?''

''Right.'' He had no idea what he'd say to Hank. What do you talk about to the strongest man you know, when he might be facing death around the corner? Ben wanted to ask him how he looked so calm. If Ben were in that bed, they'd have to strap him in to keep him still. More than likely he'd be dead by now, because he wouldn't have been talked into a trip to the hospital in Friedens in the first place.

Still, he wanted to stay. He knew Hank wanted company as long as possible. All three women needed a break. ''Go on,'' he told Claire. ''You go home, too. The guys are working on dinner, and all the laundry is caught up. You have nothing to do except take care of yourself, and you need to do that. Okay?''

She gave him a tired smile. ''Okay. I'll ride home with Carrie so your car will be here when you need it. Thank you so much for doing this.''

He gathered her in for a hug that he hoped was reassuring. She felt so good in his arms that just holding her there reassured him, too. ''Like I could do anything else,'' he murmured into her soft hair. ''Now go get some rest.''

''I will.'' She slipped out of his arms and went

to the bed. "I'll be back in the morning, Dad. And once I get home, I'll call Laurel again and let her know what's going on."

"Okay." Hank kissed her on the cheek. "Just don't scare her any more than you already have. I'm going to be all right."

"I know, Dad. Hope they let you sleep tonight."

"Probably wake me up to take a sleeping pill. Isn't that what they do in places like this?" Hank waved to his daughters and grabbed Gloria's hand, pulling her down for another kiss. "See you later."

She nodded, and Ben was struck by all the unspoken communication between the two of them. They'd been married for such a short time. It wasn't fair for them to be facing something like this already. Not that it would be fair at any time, he had to admit.

The women left, and Hank motioned to the chair next to the bed. "So come sit here awhile. Tell me about how that grandson of mine is doing in football practice."

"Sweating. It's two-a-days in August. That's what you do. Coach says he's shaping up into a good player. I hope he's enjoying it. No sense working that hard if you don't."

"You always did. Enjoy it. I don't think Claire ever realized how much the game meant to you."

Ben sat down beside Hank, wondering how to

answer that. "You're probably right. But then, I know that finishing college meant something to her, and she gave that up for me."

"True. And her mother would cheerfully have skinned her for that. I told her that the girl would get an education when she wanted one badly enough. That what she wanted the most right then was marrying you. Did she make a mistake?"

Ben's mouth went dry. "No, sir. I don't think so." He leaned forward, conscious of Hank's gaze boring into him. "In fact, I know she didn't. I still love Claire as much as I did the day we got married. More, if that's possible. Maybe I'm not the world's best husband, but I'm trying."

"That's all I wanted to hear. Things have been a little shaky between you two lately. What's going on?"

Ben spread his hands wide. "I only wish I knew. I mean, I know what's going on for me. I'm trying to figure out how to take care of my family the best way possible when my business is going down the tubes."

Hank looked a little startled. "Things that bad? If they are, why do you hang onto it?"

"Because it's what I know how to do. I'm responsible for taking care of my family, and I can't let them down."

"Son, it seems to me that you're letting them

down more by staying put in a business that isn't going anyplace. You're not happy this way, and it shows. I expect your happiness means more to Claire than the money that business brings in, any day."

"You're right. But how do I change? How do I know I'm making the right decision?"

Hank leaned back against his pillows. "How does anybody know they've made the right decision? You have to do the best you can, do what feels right, then put it in God's hands, son."

"How do you do that? I'm not asking out of the blue, Hank. I mean how can *you,* personally, do that right now? Sitting where you are, I'd be scared stiff."

Hank gave a short, mirthless laugh. "What makes you think I'm not? I'm still stunned by how close I probably came to dying today, all out of stubbornness and stupidity. Now tomorrow they're going to thread a camera and who knows what else up through my body and take pictures of my insides to see how much they need to patch up. If that's not supposed to scare you, I don't know what is."

"But you're sitting here so calmly. I'd be a basket case." Ben could feel his palms sweat just thinking about it.

"It wouldn't help any. The Bible reminds us

time and again that God knows us before we're born. He takes care of us every second, and calls us when it's time for us to go. If it's my time tomorrow or the next day, I can't change that. I can thank Him for what He's given me already, and enjoy what He continues to give. But I can't change anything by worrying—''

Ben felt his father-in-law's strong grip on his arm.

''And neither can you. All you'll do is get less good out of whatever precious time you have.''

''It is precious, isn't it?'' Life looked different when Ben tried to see it from Hank's perspective.

''Even if there's another twenty years of it after tomorrow, which, God willing, there is for me and for you both.'' Hank cocked his head. ''So, these job decisions you're working on. If you were sitting in this bed instead of me, would you make them the same way you've been thinking about?''

''No.'' It was that easy. He wouldn't give Marcy's company the time of day if he thought his time was limited. And there certainly wasn't enough time to waste wondering what life would have been like if he'd gotten a chance to play pro football nearly twenty years ago. ''No, I don't believe I would make that decision.'' He sat back in the chair, as exhausted as if he'd run sprints with

Trent and the team this afternoon instead of just watching from the sidelines.

He looked at Hank, seeing the creases and lines in his face, but the joy and hunger for life, too. This wasn't a man worrying about dying tomorrow, or any other day. And Ben wanted to learn as much from him as possible. He reached out and took both of Hank's strong, gnarled hands in his own. "Show me how to do it. How to turn things over like you said. I think I've forgotten the way."

"We all do at times, son. We all do at times." Hank grasped his hands back, and closed his eyes. "Let's find the way back together. It's as easy as a prayer. And today those are coming easier to me than they have in a very long time."

Ben knew there was a tear running down his cheek. In any other situation he'd be ashamed of it. But here it was the least of his troubles. As Hank began to pray out loud, warmth washed over Ben. The hospital room was still cool and smelled of antiseptic. Outside in the hall, voices came and went over the intercom; rubber soles squeaked on the tile floors as nurses and technicians hurried between rooms. None of that overshadowed the power he felt in this room, the love of God surrounding them both. There, where he had expected to be a comfort and help to Hank in his hour of need, Hank was ministering to him.

He knew, sitting here and praying, why Hank wasn't worried or fearful. There just wasn't enough room in a heart this filled with gratitude. When at last he could say something himself, the words were broken and stumbling. But they were all words of glory and praise for the Father who was as close as Hank, and holding them both in the palm of His hand.

Chapter Fifteen

❧

Wednesday morning, the birds were still making predawn noise outside the window when Claire got up.

"Did you sleep at all?" Ben asked her.

She sat back down on the edge of the bed. "Not much. What I got was in fits and starts. It was nice to wake up every time with your arm around me. You're so good."

She leaned over and kissed him, smoothing the dark hair off his forehead. He made a face when she stroked his hair. "I know, I need a haircut. Things have gotten in the way of getting one the last week or so."

"Haven't they just?" Claire already felt like giving in to the urge of draping herself across Ben and the welcoming bed and just staying there. But this was her dad's surgery day, and she had to hustle and get over to the hospital.

"You won, you know," she told Ben, who looked puzzled. "Our double-dog dare. It's been officially over for days. And you won."

He sat up, reaching out a supporting arm to her. "We all won. I don't know how we would have managed if we'd stayed the way we were before, since your dad went into the hospital. I'm so glad we could make things as worry-free as possible for you. This way you can go the hospital and be with your dad and Gloria, and not be concerned about the rest of us."

"As concerned, anyway." She would always be concerned about what the guys were doing at home, even now that they had gotten to the stage where *disaster* wasn't the word for the day. "I don't know who has surprised me more, you three or Peggy and Patsy."

"They sure came through in a pinch, didn't they? Who knew they could actually work together without squabbling that long? And that Patsy would have such an eye for coordination."

"That was a surprise. Now, Peggy's administrative skills I could have told you about. Anybody who ran Saturday detention that many years at a public high school can run anything."

Ben laughed. "Yes, I attended a few of those sessions myself. She did keep us all busy."

"I bet she kept you and Harley plenty busy after that flagpole thing," Claire teased.

"For a month of Saturdays. We painted or scrubbed everything in that school that didn't move." He was still grinning as he slid out of bed. "Maybe that whole first double-dog dare was a good training run for this one. Because she also made us write a couple of thousand words each about defacing school property."

"And what property have you defaced this time around? Other than the dishwasher. You got that fixed all by yourself, anyway." Claire headed toward the shower. Her head wasn't clear enough yet to understand where Ben was going with this.

"No, it was the writing thing. I didn't do any essays this time, but I've been real careful to get all the books in order during the last month. That way, when I show them to you, it will be easier for me to explain it all. And when I meet with Marcy's boss and tell him I'm not taking their offer to sell the store and the property, I'll have all my arguments down."

She paused at the bathroom doorway, feeling frozen to the spot. "Sell the store? That's what this was about?"

"That's what this was about. For me, anyway.

I think Marcy was making a different sort of offer. But I was too dense to figure that one out, fortunately. You were right about so much of this, Claire. I may have technically won our bet, but I have to give you credit for the real win—the one that counted more in our lives.''

''Didn't know I was on the team.'' Claire's words felt slightly garbled because they were mostly said against the wall of Ben's chest. He'd come to join her in the doorway, destroying her resolve to get going this morning.

He caressed her shoulders, then her hair. ''Oh, honey, you were the star quarterback this time. Should we hit the showers together for a little victory celebration?''

''Nice try, Coach. But I have to concentrate on getting out of here this morning on time,'' Claire told him.

With every hour that they waited, the family surgery waiting room at Washington General seemed to get smaller. By noon, Claire was sure she was going to strangle her sister. Carrie was not a patient person at the best of times, and the wait during Hank's bypass surgery was driving her around the bend. Carrie couldn't sit still in any of the waiting room chairs for more than ten minutes at a time. She was up pacing, or pouring coffee that she drank three sips of and then set down, or going out into the hall to find another clock because she was sure the one in the waiting room was broken.

Only having Pastor Ron from church join them at the right time kept Claire from screaming. Carrie immediately sat down and filled him in on what had gone on all morning. "I know more about stents and other pieces of equipment with strange names than I ever wanted to," she grumbled. "And I thought I knew plenty before."

The pastor took her hand in both his larger ones. "It's wonderful that you did know something before. Gloria tells me that if it weren't for you and Ben, Hank might not have made it this far. I'd hate to lose a fishing buddy out of pure stubbornness." The pastor's silver mane tossed as he shook his head. "I love your dad like a brother, but for sheer stubborn will, he can't be beat. Which is why I'm pretty sure things will come out all right in there."

Gloria gave a wan smile. "I told him this morning before they wheeled him away that he couldn't die on me. Not yet. He hasn't even finished his half of the thank-you notes from the wedding presents."

Claire couldn't help but choke out a laugh. "Gosh, if he can't die until that's finished, you guys will have a fiftieth wedding anniversary, easy."

"I know. He's an awful correspondent. I think that's why I told him what I did." Gloria's voice was wavering. Her hands covered her face. "I can only joke about this so long, though. If that doctor doesn't get out here soon, I'm going to lose it."

Carrie and Claire both had an arm around her in a flash. Claire tried to comfort her the best way she knew how. "He'll be out soon. Remember, Lisa said it could take this long or longer, and it doesn't mean anything is going wrong."

Lisa was Claire's new best friend at Washington General. The no-nonsense woman in nurse's scrubs had the unenviable job title of Patient and Family Educator, and got to walk them all through the steps of the heart surgery being performed on Hank. Lisa had spent more than an hour with them the evening before. Claire was now sure she knew about every peril and pitfall of bypass surgery. She also knew that Lisa wore a gold cross and offered to pray with every family who wanted the assistance, which was as much comfort as the array of literature on Hank's surgery.

As if summoned by their concern, the dark-haired, elfin woman appeared in pale teal scrubs. "Okay, Collinses, good news. He's done with surgery and came through fine. His doctor is supervising the chest closing, and then will be out here to tell you everything. But you can start breathing normally again.'' Her smile was as bright as if she were one of Hank's kids. "I love this part of my job. It's the one thing that makes it worthwhile." She gave Gloria a brief hug, and pulled tissues out of a pocket of her scrubs when Hank's bride started crying.

Claire felt like hugging her, too. She gave in to the desire and wrapped an arm around both women. "Thanks so much, Lisa. That's just what we needed to hear."

"I figured it was. Once the doctor comes out with his report, I want you all to march down to the cafeteria and have lunch. You know Hank won't be in recovery where you can see him for another hour. And you all need a change of scenery." She waggled a finger at Pastor Ron. "I'm holding you responsible for seeing that these women have lunch."

The pastor saluted. "Yes, ma'am. I'll do that."

"Okay, at ease," Lisa said with a grin. "I didn't mean to order you around there."

"No problem. I'm as happy to hear the news as they are. And it will give me something useful to do." Pastor Ron gathered them together in a group of chairs to wait for the doctor, and Lisa excused herself to check on the next patient and family.

Dr. Taylor, the heart surgeon, was out in a few minutes. He reminded them that even when they saw Hank in an hour or more, he would look fairly awful. "He'll have tubes everyplace, and be a color you didn't know could exist on a live human being. But that will fade quickly into a nice healthy pink, if I did my job right."

"And we're sure you did," Gloria said firmly. "I don't think I can eat anything, but let's go down to pretend to have lunch, anyway. We can stop at the pay phones on the way and call everybody we know with the good news."

Ben didn't think he'd been very tense until the phone rang shortly before one. When he heard Claire on the other end of the line, all his knotted muscles relaxed.

"Hi." Her tone of voice spoke volumes. She sounded tired, but relieved.

Ben could only breathe a silent prayer of thanks. He didn't know when he had been so glad to hear one word, one syllable. "Everything's okay?"

"The doctor says he came through just fine. We're going to the cafeteria to have lunch, per the doctor's orders. And I'm calling Laurel next."

"You called me before your sister?" Ben felt touched.

"Definitely. I had to share the good news with you first. The doctor says Dad will still look awful when we see him, but that will pass. I think once we've been in the recovery room, or wherever they let us see him, Carrie and I will come home for a while.''

"Good. You could use the rest, I'm sure. And eat something in that cafeteria, even if it's only a cup of soup or something.''

"Yes, dear. Gloria will make sure of it, I'm certain, even if she doesn't eat anything herself. The mothering urge just kicks in that way. Talk to you later.''

"Take care.'' Ben found himself breathing another silent prayer of thanks before he even hung up the phone. He went to find the guys and tell them the good news.

They were on the living room couch, halfheartedly playing a video game and talking to each other. Ben stood in the doorway, listening to them. Some instinct made him stay still, rather than bursting in to give them the news.

"I still say we should be praying for Grandpa,'' he heard Kyle say to his brother.

Trent's shoulders were hunched tightly. "You can if you want. I'm too old for that.''

Ben felt chills down his spine. Was this the role model he'd been providing for Trent? Was he teaching him that grown men not only handled their own problems all by themselves, but also were too big to pray about them? He felt two inches tall.

Kyle didn't seem to believe his brother. "You don't get too old for that. Never. I know Grandpa prays all the time."

"Well, maybe. But I've never seen Dad do that."

Ben pushed into the room, trying to keep his voice from breaking. "Trent, I couldn't help hearing that. And if you've never seen me pray out loud for something, I'm sorry." He knelt behind the couch, and the two of them turned around to look at him. "We're going to change that situation this instant.

"Mom just called to say Grandpa Hank made it through surgery just fine. And the first thing I did was thank God for that. Now I'm going to do that again, out loud, right here. And I can promise you that it won't be the last time you hear me pray."

Trent looked embarrassed. "Okay. Great. I didn't mean to put you down or anything, Dad. I just had the idea that grown-ups didn't do that."

"Grown *men,* you meant. You've seen your mother talk to God plenty. About things as small as spiders."

Trent grinned about that one. "Yeah, especially about spiders." His expression got more serious.

"Can I ask you something else? About God and stuff?"

"Anything. I may not have all the right answers, but I'll tell you what I can."

"I know you will. Do you pray about everyday stuff? Like about how things go at work, and, like, whether you caught a pass when you were my age? The little stuff?"

His question was earnest. Ben could see in his son's eyes that the truth would be important to him. "I did when I was your age. I can even say I did when I was in my twenties and you guys were babies. I took everything to God, from what size bandages to put on your scraped knees to how to help my dad manage the store the right way."

He had to look down at the carpet for a minute, afraid he would choke up. "Lately, life hasn't been that way. I felt like you seemed to feel for a while there, Trent. Like I was too old, and too big, to take my problems to the Lord. And I really regret it now because life would have been a whole lot easier for me the last six months or so if I hadn't felt that way."

Kyle clapped a hand on his shoulder. "Then I'm glad you changed your mind, Dad. Now can we say thanks for Grandpa's doctors?"

"We sure can." Ben took one of each boy's hands in his own. The hands were incredibly close to dwarfing his, both of them. It had happened so fast. Before he said anything out loud, he thanked God for letting him realize how fast things changed, and how big a part he played in shaping those hands, and those minds. And he asked to do it the right way, the way God wanted him to.

Ben had never looked so good to Claire in her entire life. Not when he was waiting at the altar for her during their wedding. Not even when he was there in the delivery room either time, urging her to last that final distance birthing those big boys.

Lying on the couch, with those same two boys, who seemed incredibly big this afternoon sitting on the floor next to him, Ben looked wonderful. Claire closed the front door behind her as quietly as possible, motioning to the boys to keep from making noise. She wanted to slip her shoes off, pad across the carpet and hug Ben awake.

Even the dog, stretched out by Kyle, cooperated with her wishes for a change. Normally he would have bounded up to greet her and woken Ben and knocked over everything on the coffee table. But right now he just whined softly, big tail thumping the ground.

She bent over the end of the couch and wrapped her arms around her husband. He felt marvelous.

Nuzzling his crisp dark hair nearly brought her to tears. She'd never take the even, tanned color of his face for granted again, or the magical way his chest rose and fell in sleep.

"Mmm. Hi. How was your Dad when you saw him?" Ben asked sleepily, holding on to her arms. She stayed there, wrapped around him.

"The doctor was right. He looks awful. Tubes everywhere, and, of course, he can't talk for the breathing tube. He still found a way to tell us all he loved us, without any words. Then he drifted back off again. The nurses in the intensive care unit said the breathing tube could be out tonight."

"Great. I want to go back with you when you visit. If you don't mind giving up some of your time."

"Not to you." She felt her heart go out to him because he'd asked. "You know Dad loves you like a son. He'd be glad to know you care enough to come to the hospital."

She glanced at her sons. They, too, looked so wonderful and healthy and strong after mentally comparing them to her father in his hospital bed. "By tomorrow Grandpa might be able to talk on the phone. And once he gets in a regular room in a couple of days, you can go up to see him, too. While he's still in intensive care, they're pretty selective about who goes in."

"And we don't go in because we're kids and we're extra germy." Kyle sighed.

"That's about the size of it." Claire found herself tossed off balance, as Tiger finally lost his little bit of self-control and nudged her side so she'd love him instead of giving all her affection to Ben. "Whoa."

"Woman overboard," Ben said, letting go of her as she tumbled. "Dog, you don't know your own strength."

Claire sat down on the floor and let the goofy mutt apologize by washing her face. "I think he does. And for a change, I actually welcome the attention." She took the dog's big furry face in her hands, holding him back from licking her again. As long as she could be here with her family, and feel this grateful for everything surrounding her, what was a little dog slobber? But just a little bit. She'd much rather go wash her face, put on clean clothes and take over the couch with her husband. Suddenly, it seemed as if they had a lot of catching up to do.

Chapter Sixteen

Claire learned to tell time a whole different way in the next two days. She hadn't divided her day into four-hour increments since Kyle was a baby. Now she got used to shuttling back and forth to Washington General by the critical care unit hours of visitation. Twenty minutes, four times a day.

Each visit showed a positive change in her father. By Friday afternoon, there was talk of moving him into a regular room on the cardiac care wing before Saturday morning. The news relieved the whole extended family.

"I know Mom could use that," Gloria's son Michael said, as he and Claire sat in the family waiting room while others had their turn visiting with Hank. There were so many people who wanted to visit that they had to take shifts to get everybody in.

"We could all use that. Even the dog has gotten used to this crazy schedule at our house, and he doesn't like it any more than the rest of us." It was true. Tiger seemed to know when the adults were leaving the house again, and made it known that he was confused by all of the coming and going. Kyle made it even clearer that he would be very glad when Grandpa was in a room where he could come see for himself that the older man was really doing as well as everyone said he was.

Visiting hours had just about ended. Claire could tell because of all the people leaving the unit at the same time. She'd gotten to know many of these people as well as her neighbors at home during the three days they'd seen each other. There were the Dubinsky brothers, in from New York and Cleveland to stay with their father while their mother recovered from surgery. Everyone had rejoiced together when their mom finally came off the ventilator yesterday.

Claire had seen several high school classmates among the families of waiting children and grandchildren. Washington was the hospital of choice for major surgery for most of the county. Ben had grumbled that there ought to be shuttle bus service from a central parking lot in Friedens. He said it would cut down on the number of tired, stressed relatives on the semi-rural highway between the two towns.

As it was, he and Claire weren't going to be contributing to the traffic to Friedens this afternoon. Today they were going in the opposite direction, for a meeting that made Claire almost as nervous as her stays in the hospital waiting room.

Ben and Gloria were some of the last people out of the cardiac care unit today. Hank's room was at the end of the long open corridor, and he kept people in the cubicle for every moment he could. So, naturally, his family was always the tail end of the departing parade.

It warmed Claire's heart to see Ben come out with his arm around Gloria, both of them laughing and talking cheerfully. Everybody was tired and worn from this ordeal, but it had all gone as well as could be expected.

"Hey, even better news than we figured," Ben told Mike as they came into the waiting room. "This was our last appearance in Cardiac Central. They're moving him before the next set of visiting hours."

"All right." The guys crowed as if there had been a touchdown scored, which Claire decided wasn't far from the truth. This was definitely another small victory in the game plan. "Want to actually go outside this hospital and get lunch for a change to celebrate?'' Mike asked his mom.

"I'll take you up on that. You all want to come?''

"Thanks, but we have a trip to make between visiting hours,'' Ben said.

Gloria looked him over. "Is that why you're dressed a little sharper than usual? And here I thought it was just to cheer Hank up with the thought that he won't be wearing a shirt and tie like that for quite some time.''

"You know he'll be itching to get into uniform again long before anybody lets him.'' Claire got up and put an arm around her handsome husband.

"Oh, yes. And who do you think will hear the complaints? Actually, once I get him home, I'm willing to put up with a lot of complaining.''

"I'll bet you are. Here's hoping you get to listen to him complain twenty-four hours a day, real soon.'' Ben led the way out of the waiting room, tracing the familiar route to the parking garage.

"Could you walk this blindfolded yet? I could.'' He pressed the button for the elevator in the garage. "At least, it won't be too much longer. Did you want to stop somewhere for a cold drink or something before we go to St. Louis?''

Claire shook her head. "Just turn up the air-conditioning in the truck, and let's motor on down there. I want to see you in action during these high-powered negotiations.''

''Great. Thanks. I'm glad somebody's got confidence in my ability to do this, because I sure don't.'' Ben loosened his tie in a gesture of discomfort Claire knew was not due just to the heat in the garage.

''You can do this. *We* can do this. If we've survived the last month with the teamwork we've worked on, anything else is a piece of cake.''

He smiled at her, and she could see a part of Ben in that smile that had been missing for quite some time. There was a confidence in him that buoyed her up, as well. Maybe that was what they needed to do more of: just build each other up. It had certainly worked during The Caring Closet opening and during these difficult days with Hank in the hospital.

She was back to feeling as if Ben was her rock, the foundation she didn't worry about. But there was a difference to the way she felt. Relying on herself for a month had made Claire aware of her strengths and her weaknesses. She knew now that she and Ben worked much better as a team, complementing each other, than they did as pillars standing alone.

Even better, that foundation she relied on wasn't just Ben, but Ben and his newly grounded faith.

The walls he'd built around himself in the past few years had crumbled. So had the ones she'd been building up herself.

Her wall had been built of resentment and hurt, layered brick by brick every time Ben failed her by coming home late, forgetting something, or messing up on a promise he'd made to the boys. She'd spent so much time and effort keeping that wall standing firm, holding on to each of those resentment "bricks." Now there was a pile of rubble where her wall had been, and it was God who had knocked it down, and changed her heart.

She felt so grateful for those changes, even though she'd had to struggle to get here. Maybe the exertion of the last month and more had purpose. Good would come somehow out of all this, even the crisis with her dad. If nothing else, she knew for certain that life was too short to hold in those petty fears and angers.

Life was also too short to spend the drive to St. Louis wearing dress shoes if she wasn't driving. Claire turned the air-conditioning vent on herself at full blast and kicked off her pumps. "Wake me when we're about five minutes from where we're going."

"Now, that's my girl. You can't stay awake in the car now any longer than you could at sixteen. If you're not driving, you're dozing. Good thing my direction skills are so good I never need a navigator."

"Right." Claire slipped on her sunglasses. "At least, wake me when you think we're five minutes from St. Louis, Kit Carson."

The lulling sounds of Ben chuckling to himself, a ball game on the radio, and the whir of tires on the road eased her into sleep as the truck rocked toward the city.

Wayne Cummings was impressive looking, but not nearly as sharp as Ben expected Marcy's boss to be. Given Marcy's style of dress and business behavior, he'd figured he'd be confronting a shark when this final face-to-face meeting took place. The man across the table was sharp and organized, but looked more open and friendly than did Marcy.

Marcy seemed to sense that things were not going to go her way. She was dressed to the nines as usual, with her makeup perfectly in place, but she wore the shadow of a pout. She looked like a spoiled teenager who didn't get the keys to Daddy's convertible. Come to think of it, that's about the way he remembered her from high school. It was definitely one reason why he had found Claire's supposition that there was something going on between them ridiculous.

Who could imagine choosing stuck-up, prissy

Marcy over Claire? Her cheerleader blue and silver back at Friedens High hadn't appealed to him when compared with Claire's wholesome sweetness. And she compared even less favorably now. Why had he even considered her business proposition in the first place? Did he feel flattered by the personal attention, perhaps? Whatever the case, he thanked God for showing him the right path to travel on this decision while it was still early enough to change.

"So, Ben," Wayne began, "I haven't had a chance to really talk to you. And I don't believe I've met your business partner at all."

"This is not just my business partner, Wayne, it's my wife, Claire. I couldn't make this big a decision without consulting her." *Even though your employee was asking me to do just that*, he thought, instead of saying it to Wayne. No sense getting Marcy in trouble more deeply than he was going to in a few minutes. She had probably come to this table thinking this was a done deal; that Cummings Business Properties had a new location in the bag, and the manager to run it. After all, when had he told her that he'd come to a different decision?

For that Ben almost felt bad. Marcy was going to look foolish in her boss's eyes, at best. At worst, she'd based a lot on this deal and would be in trouble when it didn't go through. Ben knew from what she'd said that she was the breadwinner for herself and a couple of kids. Still, she hadn't been honest or fair with Ben. Not that her behavior totally excused *him* from being direct. Ben knew by now that the only One he had to answer to, even in his business dealings, had far different guidelines than most chief executive officers.

With Christ as the CEO of any business he was to run, the rules were different. Today he came to the table prepared to be as honest as possible without causing anyone unnecessary harm. He'd made his decision through searching and prayer, and he felt confident about it.

As if he sensed that Ben was ready to get down to business instead of making small talk, Wayne folded his hands on the table. "So, what do you think of our offer?"

A copy of the agreement that just days ago Ben happily would have signed lay on the table in front of him. "I think it's probably a great offer. But I have to tell you two things up front. The first is that I'm not going to take the offer to sell my company. The second is that my decision is entirely my own, and not anybody else's fault."

Marcy seemed to be trying mightily not to let her jaw drop. "But—I thought—" she sputtered into silence.

"I know what you thought." He turned to Marcy's boss. "Ms. McKinnon has been very persuasive. If I made my decision based on her work alone, I'd probably be selling to you. But the bottom line is that I like being my own boss. I wouldn't be happy selling you my family store and going to work for somebody else, Wayne, no matter how successful I could be in the process."

"I see. And I can understand the part about not wanting to work for somebody else. I wouldn't be happy that way myself. But I still think you're making a big mistake, Ben. As we've shown you, small hardware businesses like yours just can't survive much longer in small town locations like Friedens."

"That part you're right about. I said I wasn't selling to you. I didn't say I was staying in the hardware business." Even Claire's eyes got wider with that statement. He had told her a lot already about his reservations. What he hadn't done was come straight out and say it was time to do something else.

"So if you're not selling to us, and you're not staying in the hardware business, what are you doing?" Wayne leaned across the table, looking intent.

Ben sat farther back in his chair and smiled. "I have absolutely no idea. And for a change, that doesn't bother me. I'll come to the right decision on this with enough prayer and searching, just like I came to today's decision.''

Wayne Cummings looked surprised. He apparently didn't hear prayer and business deals mentioned in the same breath very often. Ben thought that was a shame.

''Okay. Guess I've got a lot of paperwork to put in the shredder.'' He stood up, offering a hand across the table.

''No hard feelings?'' Ben felt he needed to take the edge off the situation before he left the room.

Wayne shook his head. ''Not at all. If you knew this was your decision, I want to thank you for not wasting a lot of my time in negotiations you didn't expect to finish.''

''I wouldn't dream of it.'' Ben took his hand and shook it. ''If I've learned anything in the past few weeks, it's that time is too valuable to waste, no matter whose it is.''

Cummings looked over at Claire. ''Well, Mrs. Jericho, I had speeches all prepared ready to sell you on this idea, if that's what it took to sell your husband. Looks like I can put those in the shredder, too.''

''It appears that way. Maybe you can keep them for the next reluctant business partner, Mr. Cummings. I have to say, I'm quite happy with Ben's decision. I don't know what we'll do, either, once we have quite an inventory reduction sale at Jericho Hardware. But I'm sure we'll come up with something.''

"Of course, we will. Team Jericho always does.'' Now how had he come up with that? Ben wondered as soon as the words were out of his mouth. They were all standing by now, leaving the conference room. Claire was beside him, and her hand on his arm seemed to grip more tightly in surprise when she heard his comment. Where did all of that spunk in her come from? He could hardly wait to get outside and ask her.

Once they left the conference room, Marcy said something to her boss, briefly, and he walked on down the hall. She turned to Ben and Claire. Ben could see she looked tired and deflated by the afternoon's disappointment.

"I hope I didn't cost you your job in there.'' He was surprised to realize that he really meant that. He was thankful that he didn't have to work with Marcy anymore, but that didn't mean he wanted her to suffer because of him.

"You didn't, I'm sure. I appreciate your honesty, and your telling Wayne that it wasn't anything I did that caused you to change your mind.'' Her eyes misted over a little, and Ben felt slightly panicky. He didn't know how to handle his own wife when she was in tears. What on earth did he do with a business associate reacting that way?

Fortunately, Marcy just quieted down for a moment, then spoke again without crying. "I think we all know differently, at least to an extent." She faced Claire. "I made some foolish moves during the course of this deal. I can't even tell you why I acted quite the way I did, except that for a little while I was very jealous of what you have, what both of you have, and I wanted a piece of it."

"Ben told me you've been through some tough times lately—"

Claire's voice was soft and friendly. Ben didn't know when he'd ever felt more proud of his wife.

"And your cousin Linda is part of our ministry team at The Caring Closet at the chapel. She says you're in Friedens a lot on weekends."

Marcy nodded. "The ones that I'm not working, and Jeff has the kids. It's too quiet at home, otherwise. The apartment just feels too empty."

"We could always use another hand with the Closet work. And the chapel has an awesome group for people who are working through being single for a second time. Think about it, okay?"

"Okay." Marcy's voice was still a bit tremulous.

Ben was thankful she hadn't started crying. And he was prouder than he could say of Claire and the way she handled the whole situation. What could have been awkward or rough had gone quite smoothly earlier with Claire by his side to calm him down in the conference room, and just now with Marcy in the hallway. This was teamwork. This was the way he liked things.

"I heard about your dad," Marcy said. "How's he doing?"

"Fantastic, considering. He's well enough to complain already, which the doctor says is a good sign. They're moving him to a regular room this afternoon, so we have to scoot back to Friedens and get the kids. Kyle is antsy as anything to see his grandpa."

"I can imagine. Tell your dad 'hi' for me. And tell him I really will pay the speeding ticket his deputy gave me last week."

"I will. Dad will be happy to hear that, and so will Tripp. That man hates traffic court appearances more than anything. He'll be delighted to hear he doesn't have to go to one."

The women made small talk for a few more minutes, and then Ben and Claire headed out of the building to the car.

"Could we have a little time alone together someplace before we, uh, scoot back to Friedens?" Ben wasn't trying to tease Claire too hard. Just enough.

"Sure. What did you have in mind?"

"Ice cream. Someplace where we can sit down and hold hands while we sip milk shakes, or eat sundaes."

"Sounds fun. A little sticky if we're not careful, but fun. And I'd like a little time alone. Seems like we haven't had much lately, unless it was in a car."

"And even then, by the time we get from Friedens to Washington you're not awake," he groused.

"You know me way too well," Claire said, still smiling.

"Is there such a thing as knowing your wife too well? I don't think so." Ben leaned down and kissed her as he unlocked her door to the truck.

"Maybe there isn't. I can think of one thing you don't know yet that you'll like hearing over ice cream."

"Oh? What would that be?"

"My idea for the new business. What you said in there really got me thinking about something. Let's see if it sounds as good over banana splits as it does just rolling around in my head."

"I'm sure it will. And if it doesn't, I won't have any trouble telling you so."

Claire wrinkled her nose. "Have you ever had any trouble telling me anything like that?"

"It doesn't seem so—not when it's critical. I need to get better about telling you the good stuff. Like how much I love you and how happy I am that we can make decisions together over banana splits."

"Oh, Ben, I love you, too. It's so wonderful to hear you say so out loud."

"If you want it louder, I could stand on the hood of the truck and shout."

Claire put soft fingers firmly over his lips. "Saying it to me only will be fine, thank you. I already know how loud you can shout. That's one of those things that hasn't changed."

"This is true." Ben opened her door. "Now let's go get ice cream and swap ideas. I have a feeling this will be a good one. After all, the last few you've had have been priceless."

"I feel like this one was a gift. I keep hearing the same things over and over again, and now I'm putting them together. You know when Pastor Ron commissioned The Caring Closet folks during the service a couple of Sundays ago?"

"Sure. I'm not so positive what that has to do with where we go next." Ben walked around and let himself into the truck.

Claire bounced up into the seat beside him, excited to explain. "He asked us all the questions about being willing to go where God was leading us. And every time, our answer was the same.''

"I do, and I ask God to help and guide me," Ben said slowly. He seemed to be turning his words over in thought as he said them. "Okay. I can see where that comes in."

"I think it should be the phrase over the door to the store. Right inside over the door, where the light from those tall side windows will hit it. Maybe even painted on the brick."

"And what will the outside sign say? The one that tells everybody what we're selling in that store? I assume it won't be hardware." Ben's smile crinkled lines around his eyes, but they were good lines.

"Does it matter? If the inside sign says what I think it should, we can sell anything on the outside. Aren't you the man who always told me that with the right coach, you can take any team to the top?"

"That I am. And thanks to you and your father, and even a goofy mutt, I feel like we've got the right coach again. The only coach." Ben started the truck. "Let's go figure out the rest of this over ice cream. Want to dare me to eat two banana splits?"

"No more dares. I've had enough of those for a lifetime." Claire leaned back in her seat, willing to go wherever this adventure took her.

Epilogue

January
Five months later

The phone was ringing again. Claire looked around to see if anyone else in the store could pick it up. They all seemed to be busy, so she got up from the computer and walked to the nearest extension.

"Jericho Team Sports. How can I help you?"

She was still getting used to answering the phone that way. Some days she had to take a good look at her surroundings to figure out where she was before she picked up a phone. She spent more time at the new store or at The Caring Closet than she did at home. Gloria was always laughing at her answering "Jericho Team Sports" from the church, or from home.

It was her cheerful voice on the other end of the line now. "I'm surprised you didn't say, 'Caring Closet,'" she teased.

"Hey, I'm getting the hang of this. I haven't answered the phone wrong all week. I think it's a record. What can I do for you?"

"I need to buy one of those tethered soccer balls for Tyler. He's joining a spring team, and the regular ball keeps scaring the goats when he kicks it over their fence. Do you have the youth size?"

"Of course. If you use it for youth team sports, Jericho has it. Which league is he going to be in— the Friedens park and recreation, or the church youth teams? We've got jerseys for both if you need that, too."

She could hear Gloria laughing again. "I'll just bet you do. But all Grandma is popping for here is a ball that doesn't frighten the goats. His parents can buy the rest of the gear."

"We'll be open until six tonight, so stop in early if you need it today. I'll leave a note for Trent to set one aside for you if you don't come in by the time I switch over to the church office."

"Do that. Where's the boss? I expected him to pick up the phone this time of day."

"He would, normally. But he's got the guys from the men's slow pitch softball league in the back office, planning what they'll need between now and the first of March."

"I'll see him later, then. Hug him for me sometime before that, okay?"

That was no problem. One of the most fun things about working part time with her husband was the number of hugs she got in the process. "Will do," Claire said, telling Gloria goodbye and then writing Trent a note, right away so she wouldn't forget about the soccer ball.

Ben had dived into the idea of running a team sports store from the first moment Claire proposed it. The going-out-of-business sale for Jericho Hardware had started the first of September, and by November no one would have recognized the inside of the building.

They really were a good team running this business. Ben was happy working for himself, and far happier selling sports equipment than fighting a losing battle with bigger hardware stores. Claire had a great time dealing with the different uniform manufacturers and others to coordinate whole teams' worth of equipment. And Trent and Kyle pitched in every way they could.

What told the story was a photograph of the whole family in striped jerseys lettered with Team

Jericho, and matching black shorts, that Ben had insisted they have taken where the customers could see it. Of course, "All of them" included the still-growing Tiger, who took quite well to wearing a jersey and had his shorts customized so his massive tail could poke out the back.

Claire was just glad Ben had talked the boys out of having the big furry hooligan be the in-store mascot. She could just imagine what he'd do to the displays.

The office door opened, and the league officials came out, still laughing and talking to Ben. He walked them to the front door of the store, and came back alone. There was a bounce to his step all the time these days.

"So, tired of this yet?"

"Never. Want to go to lunch once Pete gets in?"

"I was hoping we'd have lunch together. Just not necessarily in a restaurant. I packed us a picnic this morning—complete with paper napkins. I thought we could have lunch in the office."

"You think of everything." Claire gave him a quick kiss, delighted in her husband's response.

"Well, maybe not everything. But together we keep the bases covered."

"That we do."

Pete must have opened the back door, because

a flash of sunlight reflected from the sign over the front door caught her attention. The sign was even more beautiful than she'd imagined it, painted on the bright exposed brick. When it caught her eye like this, which was at least once a day, Claire could never help but admire it.

"I do, and I ask God—"

"To help and guide me," Ben finished up with her. "That was your best idea yet, Claire. Now let's go find Pete and tell him about my idea for lunch."

"At least *part* of your idea. Race you to the office." Claire took off, leaving Ben in the dust for a change. From behind her, she could hear his laughter ringing off the solid walls of their store.

* * * * *

Dear Reader,

I had to use the verse from *Romans* 8 that I picked for the front of this book because it's been such a touchstone in my life, as well as the lives of my characters, during 1999. There were quite a few times when I wondered how God was going to use what was going on in my life for His good. Eventually, in almost every case, He showed me how good came from some rough situations.

This book will leave my hands and start production in New York the first week of the year 2000. I hope that as this year unfolds you see how all the different things in your life—the good, the bad, the challenges and the celebrations—work for His good and yours as well.

Your friend in Christ,

Lynn

Next month from Steeple Hill's

Love Inspired®

LOVE SIGN
by
Susan Kirby

*Author Shelby Taylor drives off to the country
in search of peace and quiet after her fiancé jilts
her. But at a rest stop, her car is smashed by a
sign truck. When handsome Jake Jackson offers
Shelby his family's hospitality until her car can
be fixed, sparks fly between them. Will Shelby
stop writing her book long enough to see
what God has in store for her?*

**Don't miss
LOVE SIGN
On sale February 2001**

Love Inspired®